D0016483

BEST WISHES

BOOK 2

The Sister Switch

ALSO BY SARAH MLYNOWSKI

Best Wishes

The *Whatever After* series

The *Upside-Down Magic* series
cowritten with Lauren Myracle and Emily Jenkins

ALSO BY DEBBIE RIGAUD

The *Hope* series, cowritten with Alyssa Milano

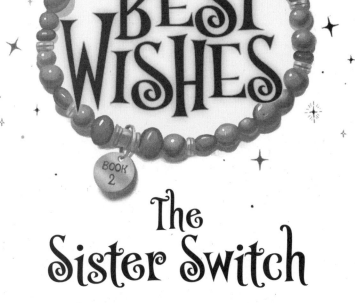

BOOK
2

The
Sister Switch

SARAH MLYNOWSKI AND
DEBBIE RIGAUD

Illustrations by Maxine Vee

Scholastic Press

New York

Library of Congress Cataloging-in-Publication Data available

ISBN 978-1-338-62828-9

10 9 8 7 6 5 4 3 2 1   23 24 25 26 27

Printed in Italy   183

First edition, April 2023

Book design by Abby Dening and Elizabeth B. Parisi

For Julia DeVillers, our friendship
fairy who magically introduced us
—S.M. & D.R.

✳

You're Not Going to Believe This

Dear Lucy,

Please read this whole letter before doing anything! Do not put on the bracelet! Do not make a wish yet!

Got that? Good. Now I can start.

Hi.

I'm Addie Asante. We've never met, but you need to know what happened to me.

The bracelet in this box is magic. And by magic, yes, I mean the hocus-pocus kind. Think fairy tales, but without the messy stardust getting all over your clothes and hair.

And no, I'm not your fairy godmother. I'm a fifth grader in Columbus, Ohio. I love music, puns, and my dog, Fufu. Plus, I always try to be understanding.

So I *understand* you must be pretty stunned by the whole magic-bracelet reveal right now, and you're likely not paying attention to what you're reading. These words are probably all blurry, so you're forgiven if you put down this letter for a sec to take a closer look at the bracelet.

I'll wait. La, la, la.

Are you back now? Cool.

Let me caution you—flashing-light warning here—*please* be careful what you say while you're wearing this bracelet. I learned this lesson the hard way.

What I'm going to do right now is tell you my whole story, starting the day before I got the bracelet.

It was Monday after school, and I was in my room with my best friends, Sloane Zhang and Leah Gibson. (When I say *my* room, I mean the room I share with my just-turned-five-year-old sister, Camille—more on that soon.) I was sitting on my bed, Sloane was sitting in my beanbag chair, and Leah was sprawled across my turquoise rug with my golden retriever mix, Fufu, sleeping peacefully next to her. My side of the room was neat and tidy, while my little sister's side was an explosion of toys, Lego pieces, and glitter. Camille wasn't there right then, no doubt making a mess someplace else.

Sloane, Leah, and I were discussing which song the

three of us would perform in our school's upcoming talent show. We were all super excited for the show this year.

"We should sing 'All Love,'" Sloane sighed dreamily. It was her favorite song.

"No," Leah said, slapping her hand down on the rug for emphasis. Fufu's head shot up, and she patted my dog back to sleep.

"Why not?" Sloane asked, scowling at Leah.

"I hate 'All Love,'" Leah said, scowling back.

I hiccupped on a chuckle. "*Hating* on 'All Love'? Now that's hilarious."

I was trying to distract my besties from their standoff, but neither laughed. My smile drooped.

"'Havoc' is a *better* song." Leah turned to look at me. "Right, Addie?"

Sloane looked at me, too, her eyebrows raised.

I froze. My best friends both had strong opinions, and because I was more go-with-the-flow, I always ended up stuck in the middle of their disagreements.

The thing is, I had another idea.

I'd written my own song. It was called "Together," and my secret hope was that my friends and I could sing it at the show on Friday.

The winner of the talent show got one month of free

classes at the Franklin School of the Arts, which offered some of the best music, dance, art, and acting classes in Columbus. Kids who've studied there have gone on to perform on Broadway and even win Grammys!

I've imagined taking classes at Franklin ever since I found out they offer a songwriting class. But I've kept that dream to myself. What if my talent didn't measure up? What if my parents were disappointed that I wasn't focusing enough on schoolwork?

But this could be my chance to win a free songwriting class. And test it out.

All we needed to do was perform my song.

All I needed to do was tell my friends I'd written a song.

I opened my mouth. I closed my mouth.

"Addie?" Sloane prompted.

What if my suggestion caused even more arguing? I was the peacemaker in the group. I didn't want to make waves. Or what if I sang them my song and they thought it was terrible?

I glanced at my keyboard in the corner of my room. The sheet music for "Together" sitting on top of it gave me the courage to speak up.

"What about something original?" I asked.

"Exactly!" Leah huffed. "'Havoc' is unique."

"I mean something no one has heard before," I said. "Something we wrote."

"No one wants to hear a song *we* wrote," Sloane said.

My heart thumped. "Not something we wrote. Something I—"

My door burst open, and my sister Camille stormed into the room.

"I am not a crybaby!" she yelled as she ran to her bed, flung herself down, and sobbed into her pillow.

Great.

My older sister, Sophie, came into the room and stood by the door with her hands on her hips.

"Then stop crying," Sophie told Camille. "And yelling! I'm trying to do my math homework and you keep interrupting me. You're *always* interrupting me."

"I was just asking if you wanted to play!" Camille shrieked.

Her sobbing woke Fufu. My adorable pup got up and trotted out of the room, probably to a more drama-free part of the house.

"Addie," Sophie said, glaring at me. "I'd appreciate it if you could keep Camille in here while I'm studying."

Camille wailed.

"But we're planning for the talent show," I explained, gesturing to Leah and Sloane.

"Well, what I'm doing is actually *important*," Sophie snapped.

I bristled. Before I could respond, my big sister turned on her heel and left. Sophie is twelve—only two years older than me—but she gets to have her *own* room. I guess my parents thought that Sophie's big, brilliant brain needed the extra space.

"That was pretty rude," Sloane said, but she didn't

look surprised. She and Leah were already familiar with Sophie's attitude.

I sighed. As the trusted eldest, Sophie was allowed to do pretty much whatever she wanted. But what did she *actually* do 24-7? Sat in her room and studied! Sure, she got the highest grades in her class and would probably go to Harvard or invent a new internet or something. But she had no friends. Mom and Dad got her a cell phone last year, and I honestly thought she only used the calculator.

If I was Sophie's age, I would hang out at Paige's, the cool bookstore-café on Morse Road. I would walk home from school on my own. My friends and I would be like the characters on TV shows starring wild and free middle schoolers!

"It's not like you don't take school seriously, Addie," Leah pointed out, and I nodded gratefully. Last week, I'd even gotten an A+ on my family history project. I'd interviewed my grandparents and written about my mom's family's migration from Louisiana to Ohio over a hundred years ago, and about my dad's parents leaving Ghana fifty years ago to come to America. I'd loved working on that project and was proud of my grade.

"Thanks," I told my friends. "Although I bombed that math pop quiz today . . ." My stomach fell at the memory.

I'd gotten a ten out of twenty. I would have to tell my parents about it later. They wouldn't be happy. I normally did well in math, but I'd had a headache and had *not* been expecting a quiz.

"It wasn't just you," Sloane reminded me, cringing. "Half the class failed. Including me and Leah! The quiz was impossible."

"Yeah," I said. "At least Ms. Frankel said we could take a make-up quiz on Friday."

Camille's sobs were still ringing out like a tornado siren from where she lay on her bed.

I shook my head, stood up, and ushered my friends out of the room.

"Why don't we choose a song tomorrow?" I suggested as we walked down the stairs.

Leah stopped when we reached the front door. "We should really pick one now."

"Yeah," Sloane said.

I couldn't ignore the fact that my two stubborn friends had finally agreed on something. While I no longer had the courage to suggest singing "Together," there was still a way to wrap up our visit on a high note. Literally.

"What about . . . 'Wild Ride'?" I suggested, hearing the

upbeat jam in my mind. "It's popular but not played out. We can do something like—"

I sang the melody—the middle voice of the chorus—mimicking the soaring tones I was imagining.

"And, Leah, you'd take the lower part, like this—" I found the slightly deeper notes that blended nicely with the melody.

Leah repeated, *"Wiiild riiide."*

Fufu was at my feet now, wagging her tail like a conductor's baton.

"Nice, Leah. And, Sloane, you'd hit the high part like—" I trilled out the chorus.

Sloane echoed, *"Wiiild riiide."*

I pointed and nodded at her. "Sweet! Now let's sing it together."

Our harmony floated above our heads and settled the tension in the air. Even Camille went silent up in our room. Leah and Sloane exchanged glances. Then they both squealed.

"That was amazing, Addie," Leah said.

Whew! Even if it wasn't a song I wrote, we would still perform in the show. And if our performance was good enough, we could win those free classes. I felt dizzy with excitement at the thought.

"We'll practice at lunch tomorrow, 'kay?" Sloane said as she and Leah stepped outside. I nodded and waved to my friends, relieved.

Problem solved, I thought. *Everything is going to be okay.*

How wrong I was.

* 2 *

Stuck in the Middle

When I got back to my room, Camille was hiding under her covers.

"Mmm," I said in a singsong voice. "Camille's not here, so I can eat this huge bag of kettle corn by myself."

"Wait!" she yelled, and poked her face out, her plump cheeks glowing. Her eyes shifted to my empty hands. "Where's the huge bag? Did you make that up?"

"I did make it up," I said with a gotcha grin. "Can you clean up this mess, please?"

She stuck her tongue out at me.

"How are my rock stars?" asked my dad, who'd popped into our doorway. He wore two pairs of glasses on top of his head. "I'm making fish tacos for dinner, but your mom said she'd pick up dessert on her way back. Any requests?"

My dad is a graphic designer and works from home. My mom is a big-shot marketing executive and was working on a huge campaign for college sports.

"I want kettle corn!" Camille yelled, jumping on her bed. "No, wait. Banana pudding!"

Yum. I love anything with bananas, and that would have been my pick, too. But—

"Sophie hates bananas," I sang in a melody I'd just made up.

Camille picked up her toy microphone, and I got hopeful she was going to clean up her side of the room. But she held the mic to her mouth and rapped her response.

"So there will be
More for meee."

It actually rhymed!

Camille posed and literally dropped the mic. I laughed despite my dashed cleanup hopes.

"No bananas, please! Get lemon meringue pie!" Sophie yelled from her bedroom next door. In addition to being super smart, she apparently also had super hearing.

"Gross!" Camille said, making a sour face. "Why would you eat anything lemon on purpose?"

I looked to my dad, but he was busy panic-searching his shirt's front pockets and his belt loops for his glasses. I gestured to the top of his short 'fro.

"How about apple pie?" I said, even though Sophie and Camille like apple pie way more than I do. I was willing to miss out on my fave if it meant avoiding another Sophie-Camille battle.

"Good compromise," my dad said, holding up both pairs of spectacles in the air and bumping them together. "And cheers! Get it? Because they're *glasses*?"

I pointed at him and smiled. Only Dad and I truly appreciate the beauty of puns. I guess you could say we're pun of a kind.

"So how was your day, girls?" my mom asked at dinner. She shifted our bright, hand-painted water pitcher aside so she could get a better view of us. The pitcher's orange-and-yellow patterns matched the African print accents in our colorful home. There were bold patterns in the paintings on the walls, the cheery couch pillows, and even on Fufu's cute collar.

"Fine," Sophie said primly, dabbing at her lips with her napkin. We had just finished eating.

"Good," I said, taking a sip of water.

"My day was great!" replied a smiling Camille as she climbed into Mom's lap.

Mom took out all of Camille's colorful hair ties and then massaged her scalp. It was Mom's after-work routine that looked like it relaxed my mom as much as it relaxed Camille. Fufu curled up at Mom's feet, watching and waiting for her turn to be petted.

"My class practiced for the talent show," Camille added. "We're doing the Barnyard Bop, and I'm going to be a rooster!"

Camille, Sophie, and I all attend St. Joseph's Parochial School, which goes from pre-K (Camille) to elementary (me) to middle school (Sophie). We have to wear uniforms to school. They're not as bad as you'd think—you can mix and match the blue-and-maroon staples with a rainbow of polo tops and whatever fave sneakers you want.

Of course, most of my clothes are hand-me-downs from Sophie. Her uniform. Her coats. Her books. And when I wear out everything, drama princess Camille plays dress-up with what's left over.

"That sounds like so much fun," my mom cooed to Camille. "I wish parents could attend. Addie, you'll be singing with Leah and Sloane, right?"

"Yup," I said, feeling that rush of excitement again.

"What about you?" my dad asked Sophie, who stood up and put her dishes in the sink.

"No way," she said. "Have I ever been in the talent show?"

"Not once," I said, leaning back in my chair.

"Exactly. I do *not* have that much time to waste." Sophie gave me a pointed look. "Maybe you should be using your time more wisely, too, Addie."

I frowned. "What do you mean?"

She looked at my parents. "Shouldn't you be busy preparing for a higher score on Ms. Frankel's next math quiz?"

My face flushed. Sophie, with her super hearing, must have heard me telling my friends about my math quiz. And of course she had to blab about it to my parents before I had a chance to say anything.

"What's this, Addie?" my mom asked, concern coating her words.

"I—I failed my math quiz today," I managed to say through gritted teeth.

My parents both grimaced.

"But it was a pop quiz!" I explained. "I didn't know I needed to study beforehand. And I had a headache. And half the class failed! Anyway, Ms. Frankel said we could retake it on Friday. And I will!"

"But why didn't you tell us?" my dad asked.

"I was going to!" I cried.

Sophie smirked. Camille looked on with big eyes. If a huge bag of kettle corn really did exist in our house right now, I'm sure both my sisters would be eating from it as they watched me get roasted. Fufu barked, as if enjoying the show, too.

It seemed like the only time my whole family focused on me was to pick on me.

"I don't like this, Addie," Mom said. She sighed and rubbed her forehead. "Lying about the pop quiz—"

"I didn't lie," I protested, my throat tight. "I just didn't have a chance—"

"Well, not saying anything is like a lie," Sophie chimed in. Sophie was all about telling the truth, no matter what. I glared at her.

"I had Ms. Frankel in fifth grade, too," Sophie went on

smugly. "And I'm just saying, she doesn't play. You can't spend every night singing with your girls and still expect a good grade."

"At least I *have* friends," I snapped.

"Addie," my dad said, his voice a firm warning.

"Well, it's true," I said. "Not everyone is a friend repellent like Sophie."

The room got pin-drop quiet. Sophie crossed her arms in front of her chest. Camille stopped fidgeting in Mom's lap. Even Fufu stopped barking.

"Addie, apologize," my mom said.

I couldn't believe I'd said what I'd said. But Sophie had started it! Why could *she* say whatever she wanted and get away with it?

I wasn't going to bend. I was always bending! Sophie never bended!

"How I did on my math quiz isn't Sophie's business," I said. "She was eavesdropping on me and my friends!"

Mom gently nudged Camille off her lap, then leaned forward to address me. Uh-oh.

"Let's huddle on this for a second," Mom said. "Because this family is supposed to be a team, all in this together. So, yes, in a way, it is Sophie's business."

"I agree," Dad said.

I swallowed. "Fine. But I'm not going to apologize."

My mom and I stared at each other. Mom's mouth was twisted with disappointment. It bothered me that her expression looked nothing like the blissful smile she wore when massaging precious Camille's scalp. Or the pride that beamed from her eyes whenever she looked at perfect Sophie.

"Maybe Sophie's right," my mom said calmly. "Maybe you should be focusing more on your schoolwork, Addie. Maybe you should skip the talent show this year."

Wait, what? My stomach flipped, and I felt sick.

"No way!" I said, pushing my chair back. "That's so wrong!"

"Let's see how you do on the make-up quiz, and then we'll decide," my dad said.

"But the quiz is on Friday," I said. "It's *after* the talent show."

"There will be other talent shows," my mom said.

"Not until next year!" I cried. I could feel my dreams of the songwriting class crash to the floor. And now I had to tell my friends I couldn't be in the show with them.

"This isn't fair," I went on. "Nothing is ever fair in this house. Sophie gets her own room! Her own phone! Camille gets to make a mess all the time. And I can't even be in the talent show."

"You can spend the extra time studying and thinking about how you treat your family members," my mom said.

"But—"

"Discussion over," Dad announced.

I got up and ran out of the kitchen, up the stairs, and into my room. I slammed my door behind me, close to tears, and stomped over to my bed.

"Ouch!" I yelled.

I had stepped on one of my sister's rogue Legos.

Camille burst into the room.

"Let's play, Addie!" she called out.

Ugh. If I went back downstairs, I'd have to see my horrible big sister and my disapproving parents. If I stayed here, I was stuck with loud Camille.

Stuck in the middle, as always.

"I don't want to play!" I snapped at Camille. "Will you just clean up your mess like I asked before?"

Her lower lip quivered. "Sorry."

My foot hurt. My feelings hurt. I lay on my bed and tried to stop my own lip from quivering.

"I'm just . . . feeling pretty sad right now, okay?" I said.

The lights flickered off, and I felt a whoosh of air blow over me.

"Can you turn the lights back on?" I asked Camille, my annoyance mounting.

"I didn't turn them off! Maybe it was a ghost!"

Normally I would have laughed. But I didn't find anything funny.

The lights flickered back on, and I burrowed under my covers, waiting for the night to be over.

3

The Wish

I was still upset when I woke up the next morning.

How could my sister sabotage me like that? I fumed as I threw on my uniform, which, of course, was a hand-me-down from Sophie. *And how unfair are my parents being? And what am I going to tell my friends about the talent show?*

"Addie! Hurry up!" Sophie called from downstairs.

As usual, she was ready ten minutes before me, shoes on, bag over her shoulder, and waiting by the door.

I stomped downstairs and into the kitchen. Mom was pouring coffee into her thermos, about to leave for work. Dad had already left to take Camille to school, since pre-K starts earlier.

"Bye, girls!" Mom called to me and Sophie as she headed for the door. "Love you. Even when you're mad at me."

"Bye," I muttered, because I *was* still mad at her. At everyone.

I poured myself a bowl of cereal and started shoveling it down.

"HURRY. UP!" Sophie yelled. I ignored her.

I heard Mom open the front door, then pause. "Oh. Addie, there's a package for you," she said.

"What? Where?" I said. I hadn't been expecting any packages.

"Right here on the porch," Mom called. "I'm not sure when it arrived. I have to run. Come see."

I walked out of the kitchen, past a waiting Sophie, and onto the front porch.

And there it was. A dark red box, about the size of a toaster, with a pink polka-dotted stripe across it. There were stickers all over the box, a stamp, and on the white label, it said my name and address.

Addie Asante
6788 Kildare Street
Columbus, Ohio 43219

I looked for a return address but didn't see one. *Hmm. Who could it be from?*

I reached down to pick it up—it was light—and carried it inside the house.

"We have to GO!" Sophie yelled as I set the package down on the hall table. "What are you doing?"

"One. Second!" I said. I used the spare house key to tear into the tape and opened the package. There was a small pouch inside, and I poured the contents into my hand.

It was a bracelet.

Pretty. Really pretty.

It was a string of purple (and a few gold) beads of different sizes. I slipped it onto my left wrist. Nice.

I looked inside for a card but saw a red notebook. Hmm. Was there an instruction manual for the bracelet? There was an old-looking piece of paper, too. I read the first line:

Because you're blue,
This bracelet is now for you.

"I'm leaving without you," Sophie snarled.

"I'm coming, I'm coming," I grumbled, dropping the pouch and paper back inside the box. Then I chucked the box inside the hall closet so it didn't get recycled.

I grabbed my backpack, shoved my feet into my sneakers, and followed Sophie out the door.

"I can't believe you brought up the math quiz last night," I said, walking right behind her. "Why did you have to blab to Mom and Dad? Now I can't do the talent show!"

She didn't turn around, but I could hear the smug smile in her words. "Well, you should be studying for your make-up quiz, anyway."

Except for the crackly crunch of leaves beneath our feet, we walked the next two blocks in silence.

Finally, with our school in sight, I broke down and begged, "Can you please, please talk to Mom and Dad so that they let me do the talent show? You can convince them. They always listen to you."

"They do not!"

"They do, too! Please?"

Our raised voices drew glances from other kids as we walked up the steps to St. Joseph's.

"You're being ridiculous," Sophie said with an exasperated smack of her lips.

"You know what's ridiculous? You ratting me out. You should help me! That's what big sisters do."

"I didn't know there was a rule book." Sophie yanked open the front door, and I grabbed it before it slammed in my face.

"There is. It's called help your little sister. Have her back. Like I do with Camille."

Sophie shook her head as we walked down the main hall, which was crowded with students. "How about I do the big-sister role my way and you do it yours?"

"That's the problem. You only do what you want to do. And so does Camille. I'm the one who always has to give in, and it's not fair!"

She huffed. "Whatever."

The bell was going to ring any minute.

"You really won't help me out of this jam?" I asked.

Sophie rolled her eyes.

"Oh, please, you're always in the middle of some jam," she sighed.

"You're right. I am always *in the middle*—the middle of you and Camille—and I wish I wasn't!"

With that, I took a sharp left toward my classroom, and Sophie went right.

Suddenly, I felt something tighten around my wrist.

The lights in the hallway flickered; I felt a gust of air. Was that from outside?

My skin felt weird. Like it was being tickled by a million tiny feathers. Wait. Was I sparkling? I looked down at my hands. My arms were covered in goose bumps.

The bracelet I had put on earlier was glowing and warm on my wrist.

My fingers looked different. Wasn't I wearing purple nail polish? Had I taken that off? Why was I wearing a navy long-sleeved shirt? Where was my white one? I looked down. Where was my maroon uniform skirt? Why was I in navy pants? Bad pleated ones! And why was I holding my sister's backpack?

Was I wearing Sophie's sneakers?

Yeah, these were her sneakers. And her . . . hands?

Why was I wearing my sister's hands?!

What had just happened?

"Out of the way!" I heard, and realized I was standing in the center of the hallway like a statue.

The hallway on the *right* side. Not the hallway that led to my classroom.

I needed some water. Yes. Clearly I was dehydrated and hallucinating.

There was a line at the water fountain, so I sprinted to the girls' bathroom.

I ran to the sink and scooped water into my mouth. My head was spinning, so I closed my eyes and splashed some water on my face.

And then I looked into the mirror.

Sophie's face stared back at me.

AHHHHHHHHHHH!

What.

Was.

Happening?

Sophie's pulled-back hair. Her serious eyes. Her frowny lips. They were all staring back at me!

I must have been dreaming. Yes. That was it. I got so mad at Sophie last night that I was having an epic nightmare.

I did what anyone would do when they thought they were dreaming.

I pinched my arm.

Ouch!

It hurt. Really hurt. The spot where I pinched stung. And Sophie was still in the mirror. I was still Sophie! That meant that I wasn't asleep? This wasn't a dream?

But how did this happen? I thought back to what I had said right before the tingling had started.

I'd told Sophie that I was always in the middle of her and Camille. And then I wished I wasn't in the middle.

Now I literally was no longer in the middle. Now I was the older sister!

"What is going on?" I yelled at my—no, at Sophie's—reflection.

The voice that came out of me was Sophie's! I had her voice, too!

One of the toilets flushed, and the stall door opened. It was Sloane. She eyed me suspiciously.

"Sloane!" I called out, relieved to see her. Maybe talking to one of my closest friends would turn me back into myself.

"Uh . . . Hi?" She stood at the sink beside me and washed her hands.

"It's me!"

"Yeah, I know it's you, Sophie."

"No! It's me! MEEEEEEE."

Sloane shook her head, looking almost scared, and hurried out of the bathroom.

The shrill of the final bell echoed off the tiled walls.

I whipped around to my reflection again. Sophie's reflection! I touched my cheek. My nose. My chin. I was really in Sophie's body.

Was Sophie in this body with me, too?

"Sophie?" I said aloud.

No answer.

I froze. Wait. If I was in Sophie's body, did that mean Sophie was in *mine*? Oh no, oh no. She was going to embarrass herself! She was going to embarrass *me*! I had to stop her!

I ran out of the bathroom. The hall was even more crowded now, and I got swept up in the tide.

I had to find Sophie. Was she on her way to my classroom?

Suddenly, I heard someone call, "Sophie! Where are you going? I'm closing the door."

I turned to see a tall teacher with a long gray braid, who clearly recognized me. She was motioning me toward a classroom.

Now what?

Was I supposed to pretend to be a seventh grader?

"Come on," the teacher said.

OMG, OMG, I guess I was.

I followed the teacher into the classroom, and she closed the door behind me.

* 4 *

What Now?

What am I doing, what am I doing?

Was I really going to pretend to be Sophie? Could I do that?

I stood at the front of the classroom, holding Sophie's backpack. *Should I go to the nurse's office?* I wondered. Clearly there was something wrong with me. But what would I even say to the nurse?

Oh, hi. I am literally having an out-of-body experience.

Students were zigzagging around me, taking their seats. Where should I sit? Where was Sophie's desk? Did middle school kids have assigned seats? Argh! I had no idea how seventh grade worked.

I was now the last kid standing, so I hurried to the back of the class and slipped into an empty desk.

"Sophie! Why are you sitting back there?" the teacher called out.

"Yeah, Sophie," said a floppy-haired boy I didn't know.

"Why is she in the back?" asked Mike Thompson. I knew his name because he was one of those friendly kids everyone knew.

"You should be sitting up here, Sophie," the teacher said, pointing to the desk in front of her. "Like always."

OMG. Sophie always sat in the front? Of course she did.

I stood up and walked to the empty desk in the front row.

Which class was this, anyway? I hoped it was something that would be easy for a fifth grader. Like art. Or music.

"Let's review yesterday's homework," the teacher said.

Homework. Okay. I unzipped my—Sophie's—backpack. There were lots of books and papers in there. But which one to take out? My heart started to race.

Wait, wait, wait. I could figure this out. I looked around the classroom. There were equations on the whiteboard.

So . . . math!

I reached into the backpack and pulled out a sheet of paper that looked like math homework. There were a lot of numbers and x's on it.

"Let's discuss pro-nomibalbinalbinal equations," the teacher said. Or I thought that was what she said. I had no idea what she actually said because I was in fifth grade and this was seventh-grade math.

And as my sister had pointed out . . . I had flunked my last math quiz.

I kept my head down, praying that no one would notice me.

"What did you get for number twelve, Sophie?" the teacher asked.

I cringed. "Um . . . um . . ." I looked at Sophie's paper. "Twenty-seven."

"Terrific. Well done as always. Can you explain to the class how you got that?"

There were a lot of Sophie's scribbles on the page, but I had no idea what they meant.

"Um . . . I can't, really. Sorry."

Silence.

The teacher frowned, looking confused.

I heard surprised murmurs. Sophie must have always known every answer and hogged all the air in the room, just like she did at home.

"I . . . I bet someone else could explain it better than I could," I said.

The teacher nodded, recovering. "Sure. We can let someone else take a stab at it. Kayla?"

Kayla smiled. "Well, Ms. Clark, first I . . ."

She went on for a bit explaining her answer.

"Great work," said Ms. Clark. "And what if we changed the variable to seven? Can someone tell me what that would equal?"

No one raised their hand.

"Sophie?" the teacher asked.

Oh, come on.

"Um . . . It's *numbernumber*," I mumbled, hoping that my made-up number-word rhymed with the correct answer.

Ms. Clark blinked. "Can you speak up?"

"Yes, I can," I started, and then suddenly felt inspired.

"But I mean, who are we kidding? I'm sure we all think I speak up too often, which isn't fair to everyone else."

There were gasps all around. The kids were looking at me like I was an alien.

Wait. Did they know that *I*—Addie—was in Sophie's body?

No. How could they know? They must have all figured that Sophie was being extra strange today.

"Okay, then," Ms. Clark coughed out. She scanned the room. "Does anyone else have the answer?"

Silence.

"Sophie, can't you help them out?" Ms. Clark asked.

Seriously? Couldn't she give Sophie a break?!

"I don't know it," I said.

Ms. Clark chuckled. "I'm sorry, I must have misheard you, dear. It sounded like you said you didn't know the answer."

A wide-eyed Mike Thompson spoke up. "She really did say that. No foolin'."

"Are you sure?" Ms. Clark asked, suddenly wobbly and steadying herself against the desk.

I hoped I hadn't given her a heart attack. Getting a pass from a teacher is a good thing. Seeing a teacher pass out is not.

A few kids exchanged worried looks.

Had I upset the balance of the universe somehow?

I had to make things right. What this class needed was one of my icebreaker puns. Luckily, I had one to fit this very moment.

"Sorry." I smiled at Ms. Clark. "I guess you shouldn't always *count on me.*"

Crickets.

And then finally a soft chuckle broke out. Was that Mike? Good ole Mike Thompson pun-derstood me.

He looked around the room, making eye contact with other kids, wordlessly asking them to back him up, and a few giggled along.

Even Ms. Clark now had a little curve to her lips.

Look at that, Sophie. I was making people like you!

As soon as the bell rang, I raced out into the hallway.

I needed to find my sister immediately. I needed to find *me* immediately.

During math, I'd kept waiting for the real Sophie to show up and pound on the door. Or for the principal to come and pull me out of class. But nothing had happened!

I hurried toward my classroom. What was Sophie thinking? What was she saying to my friends? Had she pushed aside Ms. Frankel and taken over teaching? I could totally see her doing that.

Kids were spilling out of my classroom into the hallway, since Tuesdays were when we moved to a different room for art.

Sloane and Leah came out, giggling. I clenched my fists and prayed, *Please let them not be laughing at me, please, please, please . . .*

Then I strutted out of class.

Yes. I. Strutted. Out. Of. Class.

I have to tell you, seeing yourself in person outside of your own body is the freakiest thing that can *ever* happen. I mean, can you imagine seeing your body walk out of a door? And not, like, through a mirror?

But there I was. And I saw that Leah and Sloane were not laughing *at* me; they were laughing *with* me.

For real?

Now my body was standing by the door and high-fiving kids as they left. Erin. Chloe. Zoe. Jimmy. Jono. My body was high-fiving all of them!

When did Sophie ever high-five anyone?

And my body was cheering "Woo-hoo!" as I high-fived.

I was stunned. I was a hit. Sophie was a hit!

Ms. Frankel came out next.

My body tried to high-five her, but Ms. Frankel frowned.

"Addie," she said calmly. "Are you all right today? You don't seem like yourself. You were very disruptive in class. Do I need to talk to your parents?"

"I am not me today at all actually!" my body said. "But it's so fun! I am so tall!"

What was happening?

The "Addie" I was looking at spoke in my voice, but the tone of her words did not sound like me. *Or* like Sophie.

If it wasn't Sophie in my body, *who was it*?

Ms. Frankel's forehead wrinkled. "I suppose a growth spurt could be bringing on the behavior change . . . Although your actions seem less mature, not more . . ."

Less mature?

The truth hit me like a bucket of ice water.

Oh no. Oh no. Could it be?

Just then, my body saw me and started waving and jumping. "Hi! Sophie! Hi! Guess what happened! Guess! Guess!"

Ms. Frankel smiled uncomfortably and backed away from both of us.

Other Me ran right toward me. "Sophie! Guess what, guess what? I'm Addie!"

"Is that you . . . Camille?" I asked under my breath.

She jumped on her tiptoes. Or my tiptoes. "Yes, yes, yes! How did you know? I look like Addie, though, right? I'm tall like Addie and I look like Addie in the mirror and everyone called me Addie! So I'm Addie now!"

Oh, wow. Camille was Addie.

Camille was me!

I pulled her over to the side of the hallway so no one could hear us. "Tell me exactly what happened," I whispered.

She threw up her hands in confusion. "I don't know! I was in the Apple room, which is what they call my classroom, did you know that? And I took out the blue and yellow finger paints and I was going to work on my project—I'm making a picture of a sloth and an umbrella—isn't that funny?—and then boom! There I was! Standing in this hallway. And I was tall!"

She paused to look around at the world from her height before she went on. "I was confused at first, so I went back to the Apple classroom. And I knocked on the door and Ms. Pinerette came out and said that Camille couldn't say hi right now. Which was confusing because I am Camille! Or I used to be. So I walked back to this hallway, and then I saw Leah and Sloane! And they said, 'Hi, Addie!' So then I said, 'I'm not Addie!' And they laughed and said yes I was. I was confused again. But then we took a group selfie and I looked at our picture and you know what? I was Addie! And I am! Isn't that so fun? So I think Addie and I switched places. I am her and she is me!"

I never noticed how many expressions my face makes when I talk.

I shook my head. "Camille—it's me. Addie."

She bit her lower lip. "Huh?" she finally said.

"I look like Sophie, but I'm actually Addie inside Sophie's body."

"You're Addie in Sophie's body?" Camille asked, eyes wide.

I nodded.

"So then . . . if I am in your body," Camille began, "and you are in Sophie's body, does that mean Sophie is in my body?"

OMG. She was right. Sophie, my twelve-year-old big sister, was stuck in Camille's five-year-old body!

"We have to find Sophie," I said. "Now."

"In the Apple classroom?" Camille asked, eyes wide.

"Yes!"

I grabbed my sister's hand and led her down the hall.

Sloane and Leah were staring at us in shock. I realized they'd been waiting for me—well, for Camille.

"Addie, where are you going?" Leah called. "We have art!"

"Um, there's a family issue," I said. Which was true.

"Is everything okay?" Sloane asked. "Can you still rehearse 'Wild Ride' during lunch?"

My sister obviously hadn't told my friends that I—that she—wasn't allowed to be in the talent show.

"Addie will talk to you later!" I called, tugging Camille toward the staircase.

I couldn't explain anything now. And I couldn't worry about the talent show, or missing class, until we got this emergency straightened out.

I ran with my sister down the stairs and toward the pre-K classroom.

I peered inside the little glass window. Where was Camille? I didn't see my baby sister among the kids playing with blocks. I knocked on the door.

"Hi, Ms. Pinerette!" Cam-in-my-body sang as the teacher opened the door.

"Hi, Addie. Hi, Sophie," the teacher said.

"Where's Camille?" I blurted out. "We need her! Right away!"

"You just missed her," she said. "Your dad came to get her."

"Why?" Cam-in-my-body said. "She's going to miss snack time! That's the best time!"

"True," the teacher said. "But she, well, she . . ."

"Was she freaking out?" I asked.

Ms. Pinerette hesitated. "She was definitely acting up."

A little girl behind her cried out, "Camille threw the small chair!"

Uh-oh.

"We are not allowed to throw the furniture!" another kid added.

Ms. Pinerette gave me a small smile. "We'll see her tomorrow, I'm sure. Bye, girls," she said, and closed the door.

"We need to go home and find Sophie," I said.

Cam-in-my-body shook her head. "I don't want to go

home yet. I want to go to big-kid lunchtime! Is there ice cream? I bet there's ice cream."

"No ice cream," I said.

"Are you sure?" she asked.

"Yes!" I paced up and down the hallway. "What do we do? We can't just leave. Maybe we should go to the nurse and tell her we're not feeling well?"

"But I'm feeling great!" my sister said. "Did you see how tall I am?"

I sighed. Telling the nurse we felt sick would definitely count as a lie . . . but these were desperate times.

"Let's go to the nurse," I decided, hurrying down the hallway. "Follow my lead, okay?"

Two minutes later, we were in Nurse Jamerson's office.

"We have the flu," I told her. "And we . . . threw up. I think we need to go home."

"Both of you?" she asked.

"Yup," said Camille in my body. "We both threw up! So much throw-up! Blah, blah, blah!"

The nurse furrowed her brow. I held my breath, waiting for her to tell us nice try, go back to class. But instead she said, "Poor girls! I'll call your parents."

I exhaled as she picked up her phone.

"Hello, Mr. Asante," she said. "It's Nurse Jamerson. I'm

sorry to say that both your daughters have caught some sort of bug . . . Shall I tell them you'll come get them? . . . Of course, I'll ask them." She looked up at us. "Are you okay to walk home on your own? Your dad just got home with your sister."

By myself? I wasn't allowed to walk home by myself! Not without Sophie.

Oh, wait. I *was* Sophie.

"Yup," I said. "No problem! Can do."

"Feel better," the nurse told us as we left her office.

"So we're going home?" my sister asked as we headed out the main entrance.

I nodded.

"Can we stop and get ice cream?" she asked.

I was about to say, *Don't be ridiculous! We need to go right home! We need to talk to Sophie.* Also, I wasn't allowed to get ice cream by myself. But then I realized yet again: I was Sophie! I could get ice cream by myself! Wait, did Sophie have money to get ice cream?

I reached into my bag and found Sophie's wallet. There was a ten and two fives in there. I smiled.

"Yes, Camille," I said. "I scream, you scream, we're definitely getting ice cream."

* 5 *

A Room of My Own

W e were giggling and eating the ends of our ice-cream cones as we got back to our house. I had gotten us each a waffle cone, with three scoops of ice cream, plus sprinkles and chocolate sauce.

"That was so yummy," Camille in my body said. (Hmm, I need to stick with a good nickname so this isn't confusing to write. Okay, how about whenever I'm talking about Camille in my body, I'll call her Cam-as-Me? That way you know who I'm talking about. Good? Good.)

I was feeling a little guilty for getting ice cream when we were supposed to have the stomach flu. But what if we switched back into our old bodies as soon as we got home and I never had an opportunity like this again?

"Clean the chocolate off your face before you go in," I told Cam-as-Me.

She dragged her sleeve—the sleeve of my white polo shirt—against her mouth.

"Don't you have a napkin?" I asked.

She smiled. "Nope!"

I was about to ring the doorbell when I remembered that Sophie had her own key. I unlocked the door. "We're home!" I called out.

Dad was sitting at the kitchen table, working on his laptop. "Poor girls! You two should go relax. Can I get you some ginger ale?"

"Thanks, Dad," I said. "Where's Camille?"

"In the living room. She's not feeling well, either . . . Maybe it's the same bug."

48

I bet it was. "Did she throw up?" I asked innocently.

"No, but she apparently threw a fit. And a chair? Plus, she refused to do any of the activities. Her teacher asked me to come pick her up early because she was screaming at everyone and couldn't calm down. Maybe her stomach is bothering her."

I shrugged, trying to play it cool. "I'll see how she's doing."

"Me too!" Cam-as-Me cheered, and skipped down the hall ahead of me.

In the living room, we found Camille—who I assumed was Sophie in Camille's body—lying on the couch. A thermometer was in her mouth, and a wet towel lay on her forehead.

(For clarity, I'll call her Baby Sophie. 'Kay?)

As soon as she saw us, Baby Sophie spat out the thermometer and scowled. She pointed at me. "You! Who are you?! What is going on? Why am I in here? What did you do?"

"Why do you think it was me?" I asked, my voice full of annoyance. Although of course it totally was me.

"People don't switch bodies for no reason!" Baby Sophie snapped, throwing the wet towel onto the floor.

"So I guess this means you really are Sophie?" I asked.

"Yes, obviously I'm Sophie!" she cried.

I couldn't help it—I laughed out loud at the sight and sound of her.

All of Sophie's indignation and feelings of superiority were in Camille's little body, along with Camille's high-pitched voice. Baby Sophie was hilarious.

"Do not laugh at me," Baby Sophie barked. "Are you Camille?"

"No," I said. "I'm Addie. We did a three-way switch."

She shrieked. "Seriously? So you're Addie in my body?"

I nodded.

Baby Sophie pointed to Cam-as-Me. "And she's Camille in Addie's body?"

I nodded again.

"Isn't this so fun?" Cam-as-Me said. "Look how tall I am! And we got ice cream!"

"I can see! It's all over your sleeve!" Baby Sophie crossed her arms angrily.

"I'm going to play now," Cam-as-Me said, turning and heading up the stairs. "Bye!"

Baby Sophie huffed. "I tried explaining to Dad what happened, but he wouldn't listen. There is no scientific explanation for this. Did we get struck by lightning?"

"I don't think so," I said, hesitating.

She glared at me. "At school, you said something like, *I wish I wasn't in the middle.* The next thing I knew, I was finger painting in Camille's classroom. And now you're the older sister. That has to have something to do with this mess. Right?"

I threw up my hands. "I don't know! Wishes don't usually come true! That is not a normal thing."

"Well, you better figure this out," Baby Sophie told me. "Because I do not wish to be five again. I didn't like it the first time around, and I am not enjoying it now. I'm not, I'm not,

Cam-as-Me   Me in   Baby
            Sophie's Body   Sophie

I'm not!" She started smashing her little fists against the couch cushions. Her coily hair was everywhere, and her cheeks were flushed. Sophie was always so serious and composed. But Baby Sophie was not. Next she started kicking the couch with her feet and screaming. She was having a full-on meltdown.

"I'll figure it out," I said. "I promise."

"Good! 'Cause I want to be myself again! Today! Todaaaaay!"

I carefully backed away from Baby Sophie and went up to the room I normally shared with Camille.

Cam-as-Me was jumping on my bed.

"It's even more fun to jump when you're tall!" she said to me.

"Can't you jump on your own bed?" I asked.

"This is my bed now," she said. "And you're in the wrong room!"

Oh. Wow. She was right. If I was Sophie . . . I had my own room.

My own room!

Sophie was going to kill me, but I couldn't resist.

I turned and walked right into her room and closed the door. I lay down on her perfectly made bed and took a deep breath. Her pale blue walls and stark white bedspread made the space feel calm and serene.

It was so quiet. There was no little person jumping on a bed. There were no Lego pieces to stab my bare feet. Instead there was a clean desk with textbooks stacked neatly and a pencil holder filled with pens and pencils. I stood up and peeked inside the top drawer. A stapler, a box of paper clips, and three blank blue notebooks.

I could get used to having my own room.

I took another deep breath.

Okay. Time to think. How had this switch happened? There had to be a reason.

Had I done anything differently that morning? Besides wished I wasn't in the middle? It wasn't like wishes came true *just* like that.

Suddenly, I felt a tingle travel up my arm.

I looked at my new bracelet.

It was glowing.

And warm.

Wait. Hadn't I been wearing the bracelet this morning? Meaning, hadn't I, as Addie, been wearing the bracelet this morning?

And yet I, as Sophie, was wearing it now.

Goose bumps covered my skin, and my breath caught.

The bracelet. It had to be the bracelet.

I was wearing the rest of Sophie's clothes—her sneakers, her monochromatic outfit—but I was wearing my bracelet! How? Why? This whole sister switch had to be related to the bracelet!

Where was this bracelet from, anyway?

That morning, my mom had said a package had come for me on the front porch. I had opened the package, put the bracelet on, and ignored the sheet of paper and the book that had been in there. But who had sent it?

I ran downstairs to the closet where I had stuffed the box and pulled it out. I took out the piece of paper first and, with shaking hands, started to read:

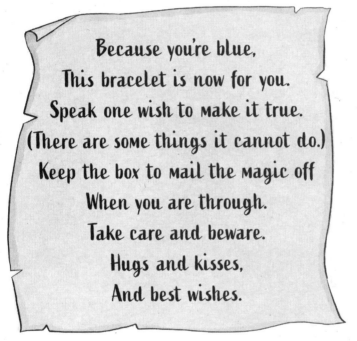

Because you're blue,
This bracelet is now for you.
Speak one wish to make it true.
(There are some things it cannot do.)
Keep the box to mail the magic off
When you are through.
Take care and beware.
Hugs and kisses,
And best wishes.

Because I'm blue? What did that mean? Because I was sad?

I *had* been sad yesterday. Sophie had been especially horrible, and my parents had said I couldn't be in the talent show.

But how did whoever sent the bracelet know all that?

I shook my head. That wasn't even the wildest part. The letter also said the bracelet would grant me a wish.

Speak one wish to make it true.

I closed my eyes. What had I said? *I am always* in the middle—*the middle of you and Camille—and I wish I wasn't!*

I'd wished I wasn't in the middle.

And now I was the older sister. And Sophie was the baby.

And Camille was in the middle.

Which meant . . . my wish had come true.

My wish had come true!

I looked down at the bracelet.

The bracelet was . . .

The bracelet was . . .

The bracelet.

Was.

Magic.

* 6 *

Becca Explains It All

My head was spinning as I carried the box upstairs into my—Sophie's—room. I sat down on the bed, pulled out the red notebook, and opened it.

Dear Addie...

What? Who? The book was a letter to me? I flipped to the very end to see who it was from.

Good luck, Addie. And best wishes.
XO Becca

Becca? Who was Becca?

I flipped back to the front and started reading.

I'd only read a few pages when Baby Sophie barged in and tried to take over her room, but my dad told her to give me some privacy. A moment later, I could hear her and Cam-as-Me arguing in my old room. I ignored them and went back to reading. Then my dad popped his head in and asked how I was feeling, I told him I was resting. Luckily, Dad was in his work haze, so he didn't seem to notice anything unusual about my behavior.

Finally alone, I read straight for the next few hours, taking a break to eat the toast Dad brought me for lunch. When I finished reading, I put the notebook down and rubbed my eyes.

Wow. I almost couldn't believe what I'd read. In a nutshell (and, Lucy, I can send the notebook to you, too, if you want to read it), Becca Singer lives in New York City. She is also ten and in fifth grade. She got the bracelet in the mail, made a wish for more friends, and got . . . *too* many friends.

But here's the thing—the box with the bracelet just appeared in her apartment building's mailroom one day. Becca didn't know where it came from originally, why the bracelet made wishes come true, or who had sent it to her. So she decided to write to me about her whole experience so I knew what I was getting into. She even warned me not to make a wish until I had read her letter.

Except I'd put on the bracelet and made a wish—out loud—without reading her letter.

Oops.

Reading Becca's notebook helped me understand what had triggered the body-switch sitch. The magic bracelet came to me because I'd had a bad day. And then I had been granted a wish to . . . cheer me up? Maybe.

But had I wasted my wish? If I'd known I could make any wish come true, would I have wished for *this*?

Maybe. Maybe not.

I looked down at Becca's letter again. She'd included her phone number and email. And told me that she would love to hear from me.

Should I call?

Now that I was Fake Sophie, I had a phone!

I reached into Sophie's backpack and pulled out her phone.

It unlocked on my face. Yes!

I dialed the number. It rang twice and went to voice mail.

My heart started pounding and I opened my mouth to leave a message but had no idea what to say, so I hung up. It was only three o'clock. Becca was probably still at school. I would try her again later.

I took out the poem from the box and reread it. I spent

some time googling *magic bracelet* and *wish* and *Because you're blue*. Nothing useful came up.

Then I tried Becca once more.

"Hello?"

She was there!

"Hi," I said, suddenly nervous. "Is this . . . Becca . . . ?"

"Yup," she said. "Sorry, I don't know who this is . . ."

"It's Addie," I said. "Addie in Columbus, Ohio. I got your . . ." I hesitated. "Package."

There was a long pause. "Oh! Yay! Wait. You got it already? But . . . I just sent it today."

"Today?" I asked, amazed.

"Yes! This morning. My mom took me to the post office on the way to school, and I dropped it off! At, like, eight o'clock. When did you get it? Just now?"

"No, I got it at like eight thirty this morning. Right before school. It was on my front porch."

"That is . . . well, I want to say impossible, but the whole thing is impossible, so who knows. I'll go with magical," she said with a laugh. "Wow. Okay. Cool. It's instant mail. Like email but actual mail. Anyway. I can't believe I'm talking to you! This is so great! I haven't been able to talk to anyone about any of this! Hi! Nice to meet you!"

"You too," I said, making myself comfortable on Sophie's bed. "Thank you for writing me that whole letter. That was really thoughtful of you."

"You're welcome. I wish I would have gotten one. I got the 'because you're blue' poem, but that's it. No note from whoever had it last. I googled 'magic bracelet' but couldn't find anything. I'm so happy you called. I'm so happy I wrote you. You sound like a kid, too. I'm ten. You?"

"Same." I liked how excited Becca sounded and how fast she talked. It was exactly how I imagined someone from a big city like New York would sound. I could hear distant car horns in her background. I had a feeling it would be fun getting to know Becca. Who else could I talk to about this mysterious magic bracelet?

Becca took in a breath. "So does this mean you read my whole letter?"

"Yes, I did."

"Great. Was it helpful? I wanted to be helpful. I wrote it last night."

"You wrote all that last night?"

"Yup. I'm going to be a writer one day. I wrote it really fast. As soon as your name appeared on the box. It was so wild! Right where my name used to be. I took out the box to figure out where to send it, and your name was on it. Wait, have you put the bracelet on yet? Or is it still in the pouch?"

I looked down at my wrist. "I'm wearing it right now."

"Isn't it pretty? I kind of miss it. Wait until you make your wish. Then it starts to glow. And gets warm! I am so glad you called me first! 'Cause you need to think *clearly*. And hard. About what you really want."

"Uh. Yeah. Um . . . well . . . unfortunately, I only read your letter now."

"Wait. What does that mean? Did you already make a wish?"

"Yes."

She squealed. "Did it work?"

"It definitely did."

"OMG. Okay. So what did you wish for?"

"Well . . . I kind of . . . can I show you?"

"Yes! Do you want to FaceTime?"

"Yeah. That might be easier."

"Calling you now!"

A FaceTime request flashed across my screen, and I answered immediately.

A girl with long curly dark-blond hair and blue eyes popped up on the phone.

"Hi!" she said. "I'm Becca."

"I'm Addie," I said. "Actually, technically, I'm Sophie."

Her eyebrows wrinkled. "What do you mean?"

"It means that I wished"—I lowered my voice to a whisper—"that I wasn't in the middle. See, I'm—I was—the middle sister. So now I'm Sophie, the eldest sister."

"No. Way," Becca gasped.

"Yes way."

She squeak-laughed. "You really hated being the middle sister that badly?"

"No! Yes. I don't know! The thing is, I didn't read your letter first. I just put on the bracelet and walked out of my house. And I was mad at my big sister, and when we were in school, I yelled at her that I wished I wasn't always in the middle and—"

"OMG. Did you switch bodies with her right then? At school?"

"Yes! And now . . . I'm here! In her room!" I panned the phone around the room to show Becca.

"And she's you? You did a *Freaky Friday* sister switch?"

"Kind of." I turned the phone back to me. "I went into my older sister Sophie's body, Sophie went into my little sister Camille, and Camille went into me!"

Becca's jaw dropped. "So you did a sister rotation?"

Ha. "Exactly."

"I can't even imagine. I would not want to switch places with my brother *at all*." She shuddered.

"How old is he?"

"Almost thirteen and kind of a slob. Anyway, did you tell your sisters about the bracelet?"

"No. They have no idea why this happened."

She giggled. "They must be *so* confused."

"They are, so I guess I should explain. And also fix it. But tell me—how long does the magic last again?"

"Until you take the bracelet off," she said.

"But I can't just take it off, right?" I held up my wrist to the phone.

"Right. Whoa, it changed color!" Becca observed. "It was turquoise when I had it! Cool. Okay, see how it's really tight?"

The bracelet did feel tight. "Yeah, but it slipped on. Shouldn't it slip off?" I asked. But when I pulled on the bracelet gently, it didn't budge. It was no longer stretchy at all. "That's weird. Is there a clasp? Did this happen to you?"

"This was all in my book! I wrote about it."

"Right," I said. "Sorry, there's lots I'm processing right now."

"I get it. And yeah, a clasp appeared at some point."

"What point?"

"When I was through," she said.

"What does that mean? How do I know when I'll be through?"

"I was through when I made a real friend. Maybe you'll be through when . . . when you want to be the middle sister again? I don't know."

"Why would I ever want to be stuck in the middle?" I asked. "And anyway, who decides? What if I'm never through?"

I could see Becca's face cloud over. "I don't know."

"How long did it last for you?"

"Only a week. But I have no idea about anyone else."

"So this could last more than a week?"

"Yeah."

"It could last a year."

"I guess."

"Or two."

"Yeah."

"Or ten."

She bit her lower lip. "I really don't know, Addie. I'm sorry. Maybe it's programmed to come off when the time is right."

"What if the time is never right? What if I want to switch back and I can't?"

"I don't know. But maybe . . . maybe just be excited. Your wish came true! Have fun! You're the older sister now! What do you want to do as the older sister?"

I looked around my room. "Enjoy my own space."

"Fun! What else? How old is Sophie?"

"Twelve."

"So what can you do now that you're twelve?"

"I can go to sleep two hours later."

"Great!"

"And I can walk home from school by myself." I started to feel excited. "And—I have my own cell phone. That's what I'm talking to you on."

"I just got my own cell phone, too! For my birthday!"

"Lucky!"

"Well, the bracelet may have had something to do with it . . ." She laughed.

From the tranquility of Sophie's solo room, I could hear Dad bellow, "Come down for dinner, girls! Mom's home!"

That was when it hit me. I'd been able to hide this secret from Dad all day. But Mom was more observant—like, Sherlock Holmes observant.

"Aren't my parents going to realize something's up?" I asked Becca in a mini panic.

"They might," she said. "But they can't undo the magic."

"They will *freak* out. I'm a little terrified," I admitted.

She frowned. "Unfortunately, that's not all you have to be afraid of."

My eyes went wide. "Whoa, that sounded creepy. Is the bracelet going to strangle me in my sleep or something?"

"Nothing like that," said Becca, shaking her head. "But there's the sketchy blond woman . . ."

"Oh, right." In her book, there was a woman who wanted the bracelet. First she offered Becca money for it; then she tried to steal it.

"She wants the bracelet, so definitely watch out for her."

"But how would she know I have it? Isn't she in New York?"

"Who knows? How did she know that I had it?"

"Good point. Blond woman bracelet chaser, check. I'll be on the lookout," I said.

"Good luck," Becca said.

"Thanks. More soon!" I hung up and ran downstairs.

My plan was to ask Mom how her work campaign was going, hoping she would get distracted and forget to notice that my sisters and I seemed different.

Mom was in the front hallway, and I threw my arms around her.

"Wow," Mom said. "So nice to get a hug from you, Sophie! I thought you were too big for hugs."

Had Sophie stopped hugging my parents?

"I got something for you," Mom said, and held out a small blue shopping bag. "An extra cake pop. They were giving them away at work. Your sisters sneak enough sweets."

Seriously? Sophie the Great got secret treats? I'd just walked into the room, and Mom laid out the red carpet. And it was covered in cake pops.

Becca was right. I was going to enjoy being the oldest sister for as long as I could.

"But you should probably wait until your—"

I removed the cellophane and devoured the cake pop in one delicious bite. Mmm.

"—stomach settles." Mom said. "Sophie! I wasn't expecting you to eat it now! Are you feeling okay?"

Oh. Right. "I'm much better. Maybe it wasn't a stomach bug. I'm thinking the milk was bad this morning."

"The milk?" Mom opened the fridge, took out the carton, and sniffed it. "Hmm, maybe it does smell funny. I'm not taking any chances." She poured the rest into the sink. "I'm glad you're feeling better."

I was about to ask my mom about her work when Baby Sophie and Cam-as-Me came running downstairs. Uh-oh.

There was no way that they—especially Baby Sophie—were going to keep quiet about what was going on.

My stomach started hurting. I wasn't sure if it was from stress, having eaten a cake pop on top of the ice cream, or having consumed potentially spoiled milk.

As soon as we sat down at the dinner table, Baby Sophie crossed her arms in front of her chest.

"There is something I have to say."

I froze.

Mom poured her a glass of water. "What is it, Camille?"

Baby Sophie scrunched up her face. "That's just it. I know I look like Camille, but I'm Sophie. I tried to tell Dad, but he isn't taking me seriously."

Cam-as-Me giggled and bounced in her chair. "Isn't it fun? It's like playing dress-up! I love playing Addie!"

My heart took the express elevator to my throat, and I got sweaty. There was no way around this. It was time to confess.

"It's true," I blurted out. "I'm not really Sophie. I'm Addie, and my stomach hurts. I shouldn't have had the cake pop. Or all that ice cream."

"What cake pop?" demanded Cam-as-Me.

"What ice cream?" my dad asked.

"I do not care about cake pops or ice cream right now!"

wailed Baby Sophie. "This is a crisis! I want my body back! And my room!"

Dad's eyes darted from my sisters to me. "Girls, are you rehearsing for the talent show?" He looked at Cam-as-Me. "Addie, you know you're not allowed to be in the show."

"I'm gonna be a rooster!" Cam-as-Me sang.

"I know I can't be in the talent show," I said. "This isn't about the talent show. We switched bodies!"

Mom's face lit up, and she snapped her fingers. "That's brilliant. Switched identities!"

Huh? "How is this brilliant?" I asked.

"It's the opposite of brilliant," Baby Sophie said. "It's a horror movie."

Mom started tapping the table. "For the college sports campaign! I've been looking for the right idea. We can have the baseball player dress up as the football player and put the soccer star in a catcher's gear. Oh, this is going to be so great. Wait till I tell my team."

Exasperated, Baby Sophie dropped her head into her hands. "I give up."

"This is extra good rice," Cam-as-Me said, shoveling grains into her mouth. "I'm much hungrier as Addie because she's bigger. Can I have a cake pop, too?"

"I need to make a quick note before I forget," Mom said

as she dashed to the counter and grabbed her laptop from her work bag.

Baby Sophie glared at me. "I don't know what you did," she muttered. "But you better fix it, and you better fix it *fast*."

* 7 *

Please Don't Talk

The next morning, I woke up bright and early—in Sophie's bed. I was still Sophie. And the bracelet was still warm and snug on my wrist.

But today, I had a plan.

I had to keep Cam-as-Me home from school.

Last night after dinner, while Mom and Dad put a protesting Baby Sophie to bed early, Cam-as-Me and I hung out in the living room. Cam-as-Me was happily playing a game on my tablet and when I looked over her shoulder, I saw a bunch of texts coming in from Leah and Sloane. My friends were checking up on me, asking how I was feeling. They had heard that I was sick. Aw. That was sweet, but Cam-as-Me started to reply with a bajillion emojis that made no sense (unicorns, lollipops, a bunch of crying faces, an angry face . . .). I dove, snatching my tablet from Cam-as-Me a millisecond before she could tap *send*.

After Cam-as-Me went to bed, I was able to watch the teen vampire TV show that my parents always said I was too young for. It was awesome.

Now I sat up in Sophie's bed and stretched. It was true that Cam-as-Me hadn't done much damage yesterday. But who knew what she would do with a *whole* day? She could ruin my social—and academic—life. I couldn't risk it.

I'd get Cam-as-Me to stay home, and at school I'd tell Leah and Sloane that my sister was sick, very sick. Too sick to video chat. Or text.

And then? I would offer to fill in for her at the talent show.

I smiled as I got dressed in one of Sophie's uniforms. Since my parents weren't letting me (Addie) be in the show, the sister switch worked in my favor. Becca's words echoed in my mind: *Your wish came true! Have fun! You're the older sister now!*

But first, I had to get my mom's help.

"You know, Mom," I said, walking into the kitchen, "I don't think Addie has fully recovered. She should stay home today."

"Really?" my mom asked, flipping the pancakes. "You

both seemed fine last night. Here she is now. Are you feeling okay?"

"I am feeling GREAT!" Cam-as-Me exclaimed, running into the kitchen. "I am not sick at all. I can't wait to go to big-kid school!"

I blinked at my sister's outfit.

She wore my brand-new yellow sneakers—the rare non-hand-me-downs I owned. Her attempt to style her own hair had resulted in a bumpy and lopsided ponytail. Plus, what was up with the extra layers of uniform she had on?

"Yikes, you cannot wear your hair like that!" I said. "And fix your uniform! Absolutely NO ONE wears a skort with leggings."

"Sophie, that's not nice," Mom chided me. "As long as Addie's keeping to the school dress code, I see no reason why she can't wear that."

Cam-as-Me smiled triumphantly.

"Where is Camille?" my dad asked, coming into the kitchen. "We're going to be late if we don't leave now."

"I'm here!" Cam-as-Me giggled. I nudged her.

Dad smiled. "Oh, are you still playing that body-swap game?"

I debated telling him that it wasn't a game, but I knew he wouldn't believe us.

I heard footsteps stomping down the stairs. Baby Sophie came into the kitchen, looking furious.

"I am *not* going to school today," she announced. "Pre-K is horrible."

"You are absolutely going," Dad said. "And no shenanigans like yesterday. I am not canceling more meetings."

Mom nodded. "If you act up at school again, Camille, you'll be going to bed at six tonight."

"I hate this," Baby Sophie grumbled. "Fine, I will go to school, but I will not finger paint. I will not! It is not civilized!"

Cam-as-Me laughed. Wasn't she nervous that Baby

Sophie would out-tantrum every pre-K'er? *I* couldn't stop worrying about how my sisters would act at school.

"What's your locker combo?" I asked Baby Sophie under my breath.

"I'm not telling you!" she snapped.

"Do you want another absence on your record?" I threatened.

"Argh, no. Fine. It's pi."

"Pi?"

"Yes! 3-1-4. Obviously." She shook her head and glared at me before heading out the door. "Please don't talk in math. Or in any of my classes. Just fix this. Immediately!"

Even the hilarity of Baby Sophie launching big words off her tiny tongue couldn't get me to shake my worries. No one was staying home today, so I had to rethink my plan.

"Come on, Cam—er, Addie," I said to Cam-as-Me after I'd eaten. She was playing with her pancakes. "We need to get going."

Funny. Before the switch, I was the one Sophie had to wait for.

When Cam-as-Me was ready, we headed out the front door with Mom. Mom hugged us good-bye and went to her car, and then Cam-as-Me veered off our porch and trampled across our dewy lawn in my new sneakers, smiling as wide as the Ohio sky.

Annoyed, I took a sharp inhale of morning air and started desperately thinking of an emergency solution for this day.

I turned to Cam-as-Me.

"I have to lay a few ground rules for you," I said sternly. "And I need you to listen closely."

Cam-as-Me did a wiggle and a quick spin, and then she nodded.

"Only speak when spoken to," I started as we walked to school. "Be nice. And whatever you do, just say no to that urge to act a fool in front of the class. And don't talk!"

"Okay," Cam-as-Me said.

Whew. That was easier than I thought. Maybe Cam-as-Me could pull this off.

As we walked into St. Joseph's, Cam-as-Me immediately headed for the stairs.

"No, you don't go that way," I said, putting my arm around her to lead her away from the pre-K section.

"Hey, Addie!" a voice called out behind us.

I spun around and spotted Leah. "Hey, Leah," I said with a casual wave.

Leah stared at me like I was a transfer student from Transylvania.

Right. Sophie would never say hi to Leah like that, or at all.

It was a reflex; I automatically answered to the name Addie. I was going to have to be extra careful. I was Sophie now.

"Um . . . hi, Sophie," answered Leah, eyeing my arm wrapped tightly around Cam-as-Me. Trying to act casual, I let my arm slide off my sister's shoulder. The moment I did, Cam-as-Me forgot all about my ground rules.

"Pre-K is down the other way, and this way is for big kids," Cam-as-Me explained. "And you know what? The chairs are bigger, the desks are bigger, the—"

She could not stop talking.

"How about I walk you to class, Cam—er, *come* . . . with me, Addie?" I babbled.

Leah stared at us. What in the world did she think was going on?

"Leah! Addie!" Sloane called, running over to us. She stopped when she saw me. "Oh. Hi, Sophie."

Sloane was looking at me strangely. I remembered our interaction in the bathroom yesterday. I tried my best

79

not to smile at Sloane, which would have made her even more suspicious. Instead, I grabbed a throat lozenge from my backpack, handed it to Cam-as-Me, and whispered, "Don't talk."

"Mmm," she said, happily sucking on the lozenge.

"Why didn't you text us back last night?" Sloane asked Cam-as-Me. "Are you okay? We were worried. Can we practice for the talent show at lunch?"

Now was my chance.

"Uh, Addie lost her voice. She has laryngitis and can't speak," I said in a serious tone. "She won't recover by Friday. She has to sit out the talent show so her voice can heal."

Leah frowned. "But she was just talking about how big our desks are. Like, a minute ago."

"Oh, those were vocal exercises. You know, like the one that goes, 'The rain in Spain stays mainly in the plain,'" I explained with a heavy sigh. "Doctor's orders. Singing would be too taxing for her right now."

Leah heaved out a sigh and Sloane's shoulders slumped.

"But I have a solution," I continued. "I can stand in for Addie and perform with you two."

There. I beamed. Not only would Leah and Sloane get their third singer, but I'd get to perform in the show. Win-win!

"You?" Sloane and Leah asked in unison, tighter than their harmony vocals.

What was with their faces? Did they think my idea stank or my breath?

"Y-yes, me."

Leah cackled. Sloane seemed confused at first but then laughed along.

"Good one," said Leah. "Sophie, you come up with a million ways to brush us off. You're so smart that most of them go right over my head. But I got that one!"

"Oh, she means the opposite of what she said," Sloane said.

Leah nodded. "Yeah, like an Opposite Day diss."

They thought I was joking. Because Sophie was never nice to them.

"I love Opposite Day!" Cam-as-Me cheered. "I'm sad today. Just kidding. Today is the best!"

"Your voice sounds fine," Leah said, frowning at Cam-as-Me.

I nudged Cam-as-Me, who resumed sucking on the lozenge.

"She's really *not* supposed to talk," I said through gritted teeth. "Right, Addie?"

Cam-as-Me nodded.

"Well, if you rest your voice enough, maybe you'll be better by Friday," Sloane said.

The bell rang, and Leah and Sloane hurried into the classroom. I gestured for Cam-as-Me to follow them, and she did.

Hmm. Neither of my plans had worked. I looked down at the bracelet on my wrist. It was still warm and still glowing.

It was still magic.

My wish had come true. I was no longer in the middle. I no longer had to give up what I wanted to please other people.

So what did I want?

I straightened my shoulders. I wanted to sing in the talent show. And what I *really* wanted was to sing "Together." My song.

I felt a rush of inspiration.

Maybe I wouldn't need Leah and Sloane.

Maybe I didn't need my parents' permission, either.

I could sign up for the talent show as Sophie!

I would sing "Together," and I would announce to the crowd that my sister Addie had written the song. And then she—I—could take the songwriting class if I—Sophie—won!

Yes!

The late bell rang.

I would sign up at lunch—but first it was time to get to class.

It was a good thing I had Sophie's locker combination, because her schedule was taped inside. Also, she seemed to be about a month ahead on all her homework, so it wasn't a problem that I hadn't done any last night.

When her science teacher called on her, I used the same trick I had for my sister.

La-ryn-gitis! I mouthed.

The teacher made a sad face and spent the rest of the class trying to get other students to talk.

I spent the whole class wondering what Cam-as-Me was doing. Was she sticking to the ground rules? And was Baby Sophie acting out in pre-K again?

At lunchtime, I rushed over to the table outside the cafeteria and wrote my name on the talent show sign-up sheet:

~~Ad~~ Sophie Asante

Act: Singing "Together," an original song by Addie Asante

It was official.

"Addie!" squealed Cam-as-Me, hugging me from behind.

"Whoa!" I turned around and stopped myself from correcting her. My baby sis must have been so relieved to see me. It had to be scary being around older kids all day.

"Today was amazing!" she said. "During science, we went outside and I dug up more earthworms than anyone and Ms. Frankel cheered for me! But I fell asleep during the next lesson."

"History?"

"Maybe? It was something about the *constipution*?"

"Constitution."

"I don't know. It was my naptime."

Hmm. Not too bad. Who didn't snooze now and then during Ms. Frankel's history lessons?

Chloe and Zoe walked by and gave Cam-as-Me high fives.

"Addie! You are the queeeeeen of dodgeball!" Zoe said.

Clearly my sister was amazing at PE. Which was funny, because I was not.

When we played dodgeball, I avoided the ball at all costs. I bet Camille dove right for it. Maybe dodgeball was less about skill and more about bravery.

"You did good." I rubbed Cam-as-Me's back.

Cam-as-Me leaned into me and pretended to purr like a cat. We both giggled.

"Addie!" Leah called, waving to Cam-as-Me to join her and Sloane. I recognized that welcoming wave and had to glue my feet to the floor to keep my legs from carrying me to my besties.

Cam-as-Me turned to me. "Come sit with us," she whispered.

I wanted to, but "Sophie" couldn't join my friends. That would set off too many alarm bells.

"I think I'll . . . sit with the seventh graders," I said. Sophie and I had the same lunch period, but she always ate in the science lab.

It wasn't that no one wanted to be Sophie's friend, I realized. It was that she didn't want to be anyone *else's* friend. She acted like friends were a waste of time. She'd rather be studying.

Well, today she was going to sit with other kids. Today she was going to make friends.

"Okay. Have fun!" Cam-as-Me ran off to join Leah and Sloane. I could only hope she'd remember her "must rest voice" rule and keep quiet during lunch.

I walked into the cafeteria. The place was buzzing with chatter, chuckles, and chewing. Funny how many details you pick up on when you're scanning the scene all alone.

You got this, Addie—er, I mean Sophie, I told myself.

I saw some kids from Sophie's math class at a table to my left. Since there was room at the end of the table, I decided to go for it and sit there. What was the worst that could happen? They'd think Sophie was weird? They already thought Sophie was weird!

I sat down. The whole table turned to stare at me.

"Hi," I said. "Okay if I join you?"

Two of Sophie's classmates, JJ and Kayla, shrugged and continued with their conversation.

"I love all her songs," Kayla said, holding up her phone screen to JJ.

I recognized that actor turned singer. I liked her songs, too! And even though Sophie wouldn't admit it, she was even more of a fan. Once, I heard her play one of her songs for hours.

"I play 'Moonrise' on repeat when I'm studying," I blurted out.

JJ and Kayla stared at each other and froze. It seemed like everyone at the table and the entire cafeteria froze, too. The silence felt like a weighted blanket thrown over my head.

Until JJ smiled.

"I play that song on repeat, too!" they confessed, a little breathlessly. "When I'm riding my bike."

"It's on repeat when I'm washing my hair," added Kayla.

We held one another's surprised gazes for a few seconds, and then we all busted out laughing.

JJ leaned in. "There's sometimes a 'Moonrise' playlist on repeat at Paige's. Maybe we'll see you there after school?"

My heart jumped. I was being invited to Paige's, the awesome bookstore-café hangout spot!

I smiled and nodded. "See you there," I said.

You're welcome, Sophie.

* 8 *

Not So Smooth

"Look who's here—it's Sophie Asante!" Mike Thompson called when Cam-as-Me and I walked into Paige's after school.

Forgetting myself, I almost whipped around and asked, *Where?* Good thing I played it cool and waved. But inside, I was squealing. I was finally at Paige's!

Paige's looked like a panel from a graphic novel. It had fire-engine red walls lined with bookshelves and covered with posters of superheroes. There was a café in the corner selling drinks, and the place was packed.

The seventh and eighth graders standing in line all glanced at me. Sophie never went to Paige's. They looked surprised but . . . kinda pleasantly surprised? I couldn't say for sure. Older kids are harder to read.

"Hey," I said to Mike as I got in line behind him. Cam-as-Me had been staring so hard at the menu of icy drinks that she clipped my heels and slammed into me. I wobbled but kept us from tumbling to the floor.

"Nice reflexes," said Mike, sounding impressed.

"Thanks," I said as casually as possible. My heart was galloping like a wild horse because I'd just narrowly avoided making a fool out of myself.

Mike was right. Sophie's body was quick. I remembered she used to play soccer when she was younger. That was back before she got so serious about . . . everything.

Mike flashed Cam-as-Me his signature friendly smile. "How did you convince Sophie to stop by?"

Cam-as-Me didn't hesitate. "She's treating me to a smoothie!"

"You trying to win a best big sis award?" Mike asked me.

"I totally am," I said.

He laughed. "I don't know about that. My big sister is pretty dope."

"I have two big sisters." Cam-as-Me bounced on her toes and stuck two fingers in the air. Mike looked confused. "But one of them is not so big right now. She's—"

"Next!" the cashier interrupted just in time.

I ordered a hot tea with honey to protect my singing voice. Cam-as-Me got a strawberry-banana smoothie. The two of us sipped our drinks and browsed the bookshelves. I noticed Mike, JJ, Kayla, and a few other seventh graders taking their drinks to one of the outdoor tables.

Should I join them? Maybe I should! I motioned for Cam-as-Me to follow me outside.

It was a sunny afternoon, so walkers, runners, and bikers were making their way down the winding paths leading into Buckeye Forest Park. When Camille was tiny, Sophie and I had taken her toddling along that trail. Look at my baby sister now—blazing trails as a fifth grader!

But at that moment, baby sis was about to leave me behind.

Cam-as-Me had started skipping toward home. I glanced at JJ and Kayla, but then I waved to them and hurried after Cam-as-Me. Sophie would have to make friends another time.

"Watch where you're going," I called to Cam-as-Me when she almost bumped into a passerby. Something in my sister's carefree swagger made me a tiny bit jealous. Imagine skipping down the sidewalk and being that unbothered by what people thought of you.

I guessed I spent a lot of time acting how other people expected me to. Cam-as-Me wasn't worried about expectations. She wasn't focused on the stares she was getting from people on the sidewalk. She was only focused on her joy. That was pretty cool. And surprisingly, her joy looked pretty cool on *me*!

"Hey, wait for me!" I said, jogging to catch up.

And that's when I saw it—a flash of yellow from behind a large tree.

Huh? What was that?

I paused to look, but whatever I'd seen was gone. Strange.

"Come on, Sissy!" Cam-as-Me bounced in place.

That flash of yellow appeared again. This time I realized I was seeing blowy strands of blond hair. There was a woman standing behind a tree. A blond woman who was openly staring at me. Shivers ran down my spine. There was something about her . . .

"L-let's cross the street," I said, grabbing Cam-as-Me's hand and zipping across Mill Street once there was no traffic.

The lurking lady stayed on her side of the street, but she continued following us, moving from tree to tree. I didn't see her actually switch from one tree to the other, but somehow, she'd just appear behind the next tree a second later.

"How is she doing that?" I asked, confused.

"What's going on?" Cam-as-Me asked, giggling. "Are we playing hide-and-seek?"

"Sort of," I said, yanking Cam-as-Me and hiding with her behind a large oak. "Two can play that game."

Cam-as-Me was all too happy to wait quietly behind the large trunk. I peeked across the street, on the lookout for the blond woman.

Then it hit me. Could this be the woman Becca had warned me about? There was only one way to find out for sure.

I pulled out my phone, ready to snap a picture the next time the blond woman ran from one tree to the other. The only thing was, she didn't run. When she thought we weren't looking, she rolled out on clunky roller skates.

Huh?

With her arms flailing over her head in the wackiest herky-jerky movements I'd ever seen, she careened to the next tree. I saw then that the tree wasn't so much her hiding spot as her brake. She didn't have enough control of her roller skates to stop without the help of the tree.

When her face was in full view, I zoomed in and snapped a few pics before texting them to Becca.

Luckily, Becca responded right away.

That's her!!! The blond woman who is after the bracelet!

I couldn't believe it. This woman had shown up all the way from New York City? And on roller skates?

Creepy. But also kind of funny.

"Hey, girls!" the blond woman shouted. She was trying to make her way to the curb now. She drifted down a driveway slope and started rolling into the street. "Wait up. I want to ask you someth— *Whooooaaa!*"

HONK!

An approaching car slowed just in time. The blond woman swerved away and back to a tree, which she hugged in fear.

"Maybe these skates weren't the best idea," she huffed.

"Let's get out of here," I told my sister, grabbing her hand. We ran down the street and around the corner.

I kept looking over my shoulder until I was sure the blond woman was no longer following us. I didn't want her to know where we lived.

"I think we lost her," I said, out of breath.

Cam-as-Me clapped. "That was so much fun!"

I shook my head. "If you say so."

There was no need to scare Cam-as-Me. The blond woman was weird, but she wasn't as scary as Becca described. I chuckled to myself thinking of how goofy she'd looked on skates.

My phone buzzed. It was Becca.

Becca: Is she still there?

Me: No. We got away in time.

Becca: Oh good. Nice job!

Hopefully the blond woman would roll down a never-ending hill and that would be the last we'd see of her.

When we were safely home, we found Dad making dinner and Baby Sophie in the living room, watching a robotics competition on TV. I definitely wanted to avoid Baby Sophie, but Cam-as-Me went to join her and demanded to watch cartoons. As the two of them argued, I took that opportunity to slip upstairs.

I had something to do.

I walked into my old bedroom and sat down at my keyboard so I could practice singing "Together." I had to get myself ready to shine on Friday.

It was funny being in my room again. I realized I maybe missed it a little.

I was reviewing the "Together" sheet music when Baby Sophie stomped into the room.

"We need to talk," she barked at me in her cute little voice.

"I'm busy," I said as pleasantly as possible. Didn't want to poke the baby bear with the mama-bear-sized anger.

"I don't care," Baby Sophie said.

"What do you need?"

"I need you to tell me why I'm in this predicament!"

Aw, hearing such a big word come out in a little voice was soooooo adorable.

"What are you smiling about?" Baby Sophie growled. The little finger pointing menacingly at me was smeared in an array of colors. "I had the most ridiculous day! I had to finger paint! And the other kids in the class are monsters. They eat Play-Doh!"

"I-I'm sorry about that," I said, inching away from her finger.

"Don't be sorry. DO something. Get me back in my body!" Baby Sophie was screeching now.

"What can I do?" I asked, fumbling nervously with the bracelet.

Baby Sophie stared at my wrist. "Wait. What is that bracelet? Why am I wearing it? Does it have to do with what's going on?"

Before I could answer, Baby Sophie lunged at my wrist.

"Gimme that bracelet!" she shouted in fury.

She pulled and yanked on it. But the bracelet didn't come off.

"Why is it so tight?" she asked.

"It just is."

"There's no clasp?"

"No," I said. "It won't come off."

"I don't believe you!" she cried, jumping on me like a pouncing cat. I fell off the keyboard bench, my funny bone narrowly missing my bookcase.

"Calm down!" I shouted, scrambling to my hands and knees. "We'll figure this out."

Sophie took advantage of me being lower to the floor, and she belly flopped onto my back. "I want it now!"

I felt like I was wearing a human cape. Every time I struggled to get on my feet, Baby Sophie yanked me onto my knees.

"The bracelet—doesn't—come—off!" I repeated between attempts to stand.

"Girls, what in the world is going on here?"

I hadn't even heard Mom come into the room.

"Camille, what's gotten into you?" she gasped. "Daddy told me about your behavior this afternoon, and I couldn't believe my ears."

I felt the squirmy weight lift off my back as Mom picked up Baby Sophie.

"Sophie," Mom said to me. "Why are you in here?"

Oh, right. Before I could come up with an excuse, Baby Sophie lunged for me again.

"Gimme that bracelet!" she cried.

Mom frowned. "You want a bracelet like Sophie's? The

last one you had, you lost on the playground, remember?" Mom crouched down to Baby Sophie, face-to-face. That was brave.

"*I* did not lose it!" Baby Sophie hollered. "Camille did!"

Mom sighed. "This identity swap game may be too much for you," she told Baby Sophie. "Come on, let's give you a warm bath so you can go to bed early." She scooped up Baby Sophie again and carried her out the door.

"But I'm not even tired! This isn't over!" Baby Sophie yelled at me.

I let out a breath. Mom had been so distracted by Baby Sophie that she hadn't thought to ask where I'd gotten my new bracelet.

I sat back down on the keyboard bench. Time to focus on singing.

I hit record on the voice app on Sophie's phone so I could sing the first few lines of "Together" and hear how I sounded.

I closed my eyes and sang from the heart.

"Through the stormy weather,

Let's stay close together.

When the chips are stacked,

We'll have each other's back . . ."

I played back the recording and gave my performance a listen.

Wait. Who was that warbling in my ears? My voice was piercing and way off-key. It sounded nothing like when I sang in church or when I sang with my friends.

Why did I sound so horrible?

Ugh. I realized it then. I was in Sophie's body, so I had her voice. That meant I sang how *she* sang. Sophie was never one to belt a song, so I'd never really heard her singing voice.

Now I knew for sure: My plan to sing in the talent show wouldn't work.

But then I had another thought. If *I* didn't have the vocal skills to be in the talent show, that meant Cam-as-Me did!

Original mission scrapped. New plan: Get Cam-as-Me to perform with Sloane and Leah.

If Cam-as-Me won, then I would get the free class! Assuming I switched back eventually.

I *would* switch back eventually, wouldn't I?

Now I just had to get my parents to let Cam-as-Me perform. Which meant I had to do what Sophie couldn't do for me: Go to bat for my kid sister and ask my parents to give her—well, me—a second chance.

* 9 *

Pretty, Pretty Please

"Mom, Dad, can I talk to you?" I asked, walking into their home office after dinner.

Dad took off his glasses and placed them on top of his head, next to the pair that was already there. "Sure, Sophie. What's up?"

Mom looked up from her laptop screen. "If it's about Camille acting out earlier, I had a talk with her, and you should expect an apology in the morning. She fell fast asleep! The poor girl exhausted herself."

"Well, I was thinking," I said, leaning against Mom's desk, "Addie had a point the other day. Maybe I've been studying too hard and that's why I haven't really . . . made many friends."

My parents exchanged confused glances. I guessed

they'd never heard Sophie admit to studying too much. Or to any imperfections.

"I know that's not something I say every day," I added. "But I should have been in Addie's corner. She's really upset that she can't sing in the talent show. And it's because of me."

Mom reached across her desk to touch my hand. "Addie isn't missing the talent show because of you. She didn't tell us about failing her math quiz. And she refused to apologize to you. Her behavior wasn't right."

"Exactly," Dad said.

"And I have to say," Mom went on, "she hasn't seemed very diligent about studying for her make-up quiz."

"And she doesn't seem that upset," Dad chimed in.

From the living room, we could hear Cam-as-Me happily stomping around as she watched a cartoon musical on TV.

I'd forgotten about the math quiz. How was Cam-as-Me going to pass it? Argh, I had to focus on one thing at a time. Talent show first.

"Addie regrets her decision and has apologized to me for the things she said that night. And now she's . . . um . . . grief-dancing to a cartoon," I added hastily. "I want her to have a second chance. Can she be in the talent show? It would make her happy, and that would make me happy. And I can even help her study for the math quiz!" I finished.

Was that too much? My parents *were* looking at me a little strangely.

Maybe I should quit while I was ahead. Sophie wasn't one to beg or linger on a topic. "I'll let you think on this," I told my parents. "I'll head out to walk Fufu. Be back soon."

I left the office before they had the chance to ask any more questions.

I grabbed the braided dog leash hanging on the lime-green hook near our front door. "Fufu, c'mere, girl!" I called out.

Fufu ran to me and licked my hand. She wasn't usually that affectionate with Sophie. It was as if she had a sense I was really Addie. Pets are magical in that way.

I hooked Fufu's leash to her collar, and we stepped

outside into the cool evening. Fufu led me to her favorite tree—the one with slender branches extending like dainty fingers plucking a cloud from the sky. It was in front of our house, so I was glad we didn't have to walk far. I was eager to go back inside and see if my parents had come to a decision about the talent show.

"Hi there," said a voice from behind the tree. I gave a start. It was the blond woman!

She came roller-skating clumsily onto the sidewalk.

I froze, but Fufu's tail began to wag excitedly. Some guard dog.

The woman wobbled over to pet Fufu, but I tugged the leash and backed away before she could get at her.

"What do you want?" I asked her. "How did you know where I live?"

She tried to roll back to the tree but landed her knees on the patch of grass. "I really thought these skates would work," she muttered. She used the tree's support to get back on her feet—er, wheels. "I can track wherever the bracelet is," she said between labored breaths.

She was tracking me? I looked for a microchip in the bracelet beads, but there wasn't one as far as I could tell.

"I don't know what's happening, or how you're finding me, but you need to stay away!" I shouted, yanking on

Fufu's leash. I ran back to my front door and into my house, and locked the door behind me.

"Sophie?" Mom said, making me jump. She'd just walked into the front hall.

"Yes?" I answered, surprised to hear my voice sounded so steady.

"We've been thinking about what you said, and you're right. We told Addie she could participate in the talent show if she wants to."

Yes! "Thank you!" I called out.

I ran into the living room, where Cam-as-Me was playing a game on my tablet.

I gently pulled the tablet from her hands and sent a text to Leah and Sloane:

Me: My voice is better. I can perform on Friday!
Sloane: YESSSSSSSSSS
Leah: Practice tomorrow at lunch?
Me: 👍

I handed the tablet back to Cam-as-Me and beamed.

"You're going to be in the talent show!" I exclaimed.

"I know," Cam-as-Me said. "Mommy told me! And I'm going to dress up as a rooster to sing, 'Cock-a-doodle—'"

"*No!*" I interrupted, waving my hands. "You're not doing the rooster. I need to teach you the lyrics to 'Wild Ride' so you can rehearse with Leah and Sloane tomorrow. Okay? High five!"

Cam-as-Me grinned and slapped my palm. "Let's do this!"

As I pulled up the lyrics on my tablet, I smiled. And I tried to forget about the scary blond woman who wanted the bracelet.

* 10 *

Food, Food Everywhere

The next morning, I was in Sophie's science class when I looked out the window.

Then I did a double take.

Baby Sophie was in the schoolyard, Hula-Hooping.

Yes. Hula-Hooping.

I didn't even know Sophie knew how to Hula-Hoop.

Study—yes. Boss me around—absolutely. Hula-Hoop? No.

Her whole class was outside, every kid doing different activities. It was their recess. Baby Sophie had a red Hula-Hoop around her waist, and it was going round and round and not falling.

And the most unexpected part? She was smiling! She was having *fun*!

I covered my mouth to stop myself from cheering. Maybe the sister switch wasn't the worst thing for Sophie. Maybe in the future she'd take Hula-Hoop study breaks . . . Maybe she'd enter the Hula-Hooping book of world records!

Nah, that was probably taking it too far.

"Excited about something, Sophie?"

I tore my gaze away from the window to see my teacher studying me.

I gestured awkwardly outside. "Uh, it's just . . . the Hula-Hoops—"

"Perfect observation!" shouted Ms. Alston. "Great example of a real-life scientific equation: The size of the Hula-Hoops affect the speed they rotate. Well done, Sophie!"

I was relieved but also kinda annoyed. Even when caught daydreaming, Sophie still got praised.

Finally, it was time for lunch.

As I walked into the cafeteria, I spotted Cam-as-Me in a corner rehearsing with Sloane and Leah. The three of them were laughing. Seeing them together—so happy—stung. Especially because I'd just scratched Sophie's name from the talent show sign-up sheet. I was glad Cam-as-Me was doing her part to stick with the talent show plan. But my friends didn't seem to care that I wasn't my normal self. In fact, they were laughing harder than they usually did.

Did my friends like my kid sister better than me?

I walked over to the table I'd sat at the day before. JJ and Kayla nodded at me when I joined them, which made me feel better. Another classmate, Mandy, even flashed me a polite smile.

Look, Sophie! I made you friends! Well, not friends friends. More like table friends.

"It's going to be so much fun," JJ was saying.

"No one will expect it!" Kayla said.

"We are going to crush it," JJ added.

"Crush what?" I asked.

"The talent show," Mandy said.

Oh! "What are you guys doing?" I asked, opening my milk carton.

"It's a secret," Mandy said.

I felt my cheeks heat up. Maybe we weren't table friends after all. "Sorry. Never mind."

"It's more of a surprise," Kayla added.

I wished I was doing something for the talent show. I wished Sophie's voice could carry a tune.

Suddenly, loud singing came from the other side of the cafeteria.

What was that?

I looked up to see ten fifth graders doing a dance in the middle of the cafeteria.

Led by Cam-as-Me.

What was she doing?

"Flash mob!" someone yelled.

"Oh no." My heart took the express elevator to my throat. There "I" was in the middle of the cafeteria doing a two-step, then slide to the right, and then another two-step and slide to the left. My arms were swaying above my head, and I had the goofiest grin on my face. Oh no, no, no, no. What was everyone going to think of me?

Why couldn't Cam-as-Me just lie low? You wouldn't borrow someone's favorite white dress and belly flop into a mud pit. You wouldn't play catch with a borrowed cell phone. Cam-as-Me was only temporarily in my body (hopefully). And yet she had to make herself the center of attention at all times!

The other fifth graders were cheering, but the sixth graders started laughing and pointing. Didn't my sister realize people were making fun of her?

Still holding my milk, I stormed over to where she was dancing and took her arm. "Stop!" I said.

Cam-as-Me looked startled for a second and then

dissolved into giggles as she pointed at me. "You look like Sophie more than ever right now. All disappointed."

I knew the exact face she was talking about. I dreaded that look of Sophie's. It made me feel bad about myself.

I couldn't let that distract me. "You need to stop! Everyone is looking!"

"Then wave!" she giggled.

"This is awesome!" Sloane said, and did a spin.

Cam-as-Me spun, too. I tried to grab her arm again, but she knocked into me by mistake.

Which made my milk go flying.

All over Cam-as-Me.

She smiled wickedly, and before I could blink, she'd picked up her leftover sandwich and tossed it at my face.

Then she yelled, "Foooooooooood fight!"

There was a second of silence.

And then everyone lost it.

Sandwiches were thrown. Drinks were tossed. Every kid in the cafeteria was either flinging food or hiding under the table. Within twenty seconds, the scene had gone from flash mob to total chaos.

I stood there, in shock. Until Mike tossed a piece of pepperoni at my shirt. I thought fast and tossed a container of applesauce back at him.

"Nice aim, Sophie!" he yelled.

And then there was a loud teacher whistle. Which everyone ignored.

Then there were two teachers standing on lunch tables blowing whistles.

"Stop this right now!" Mr. Collins yelled.

A lone piece of pizza arced across the room and landed with a *splat*.

"NOW!" he boomed.

We all froze.

"Who started this?" he asked.

All eyes turned to me and my sister.

"I've never been to the principal's office before," Cam-as-Me said as we walked down the hall. Well, I was walking. She was skipping. I think she found this fun.

"I've never been, either," I said. And certainly Sophie—the real Sophie—*never* had.

Cam-as-Me and I sat down on the bench outside Principal Bryant's office to wait for her to call us inside.

Unfortunately, the pre-K classroom was across the hall from the principal's office.

Double unfortunately, Baby Sophie chose that moment

to leave the classroom, her fingers covered in paint. She was probably on her way to wash her hands.

"Why are you two here?" she asked, coming to an abrupt halt.

"We had a food fight," Cam-as-Me announced. "There was flying pizza! It was great."

"And you got sent to the principal's office?" she asked, her eyes widening with shock.

"Yes! I can't wait to see what it looks like in there!" Cam-as-Me said.

Baby Sophie's face crumpled. "Addie! What is wrong with you?"

"It wasn't my fault!" I said, gesturing to Cam-as-Me. "She started it."

"What if it goes on my permanent record?" Baby Sophie screeched. "You two are ruining everything!"

Baby Sophie was right. I'd felt the same way when I watched Cam-as-Me leading the flash mob.

Just then, Ms. Pinerette, Camille's teacher, opened the door and looked at Baby Sophie. "Is everything okay, Camille? I can hear you screaming. Remember your indoor voice! And please hurry, pickup is any minute."

"I am furious at my sisters!" Baby Sophie screamed.

"Look at them! They are a mess! They are covered in tomato sauce and milk!"

Cam-as-Me took that as a cue to peel a slimy spaghetti noodle off her shirt and hurl it at Baby Sophie. It landed right on her head and hung down her forehead.

"Are you kidding me? Are you kidding me?" Baby Sophie ran straight toward Cam-as-Me and started rubbing her hands on her, getting the finger paint all over her uniform.

"Stop it!" I hollered. And the next thing I knew, both of them were rubbing their spaghetti sauce and painty hands all over *my* uniform.

"Girls!" Ms. Pinerette called. "Stop that this instant!"

"What is happening?" Principal Bryant asked, finally opening her door.

We heard our dad's voice next. "Addie! Camille! *Sophie!* What's gotten into the three of you?"

We have gotten into each other, I answered to myself. But I couldn't say that out loud.

I dropped my hands and turned around to see all the pre-K parents, including my dad, staring at the three of us, their mouths agape.

Now we were *really* in trouble.

We got a lecture from Principal Bryant and were told that we would have to help clean up the cafeteria.

"This is no way for siblings to treat one another," she said, clucking her tongue. "You have to learn to be a team."

Dad glared at us.

"We'll talk about this later," he said.

Baby Sophie headed home with Dad, leaving Cam-as-Me and yours truly to clean the cafeteria and then finish out the humiliating day in our stained, smelly uniforms.

＊ 11 ＊

Surprise Visitor

When Cam-as-Me and I got home, Mom was waiting for us. Dad must have called her to come home from work early because of all the drama.

Mom's jaw dropped at the sight of me and my sister. She looked like she wanted to toss us into the washing machine, along with our clothes.

"You two are just as bad as Camille," said Mom.

"Hey!" Cam-as-Me said.

"Addie, you shower first," Mom ordered, and Cam-as-Me obediently headed for the stairs. "Camille is napping, so be quiet."

Exhausted, I started for the stairs, too. I was looking forward to the quiet comfort of "my" bedroom.

"Not so fast, Sophie," said Mom. "We need to have a word."

I knew that tone. Mom was revving up for a lecture. My mind started racing. But Sophie never got lectured. Right? Maybe this was going to be more of a consultation. Yeah. My parents probably always consulted with Sophie about how best to ground me and Camille. That was it.

But when I glanced at Mom, her eyes looked like lasers. Uh-oh.

I could hear my dad's muffled voice coming from his office, so I knew he was on a work call. Dad was more relaxed than Mom—if he was involved in a lecture, it usually wasn't as bad. But right now it was all Mom and me.

"Starting a food fight?" Mom snapped right away. "Getting sent to the principal's office? Do you want to be known as a kid who gets into trouble? Those kids have to work extra hard to earn back trust. What have I always told you over the years? You need to set an example for your sisters. What message is a food fight sending them? That it's okay to deface school property? That it's okay to get into trouble? Nope. No, ma'am. I expected more from you, Sophie. I really did."

I was in shock. "I . . . I'm sorry."

"You should be. As the oldest, everything you do reflects on your sisters. I don't want this kind of behavior to ever happen again, you hear?"

I nodded and hung my head. "I'm really sorry."

"Now go on and clean yourself up."

I turned and headed upstairs with a lump in my throat. My mom had never spoken to me—to Addie—like that. She never made me feel like I had to set a good example.

I only had to be me.

As I got into the shower, I thought of that quote from *Spider-Man*. With great power came great responsibility. I guess it was like that with Sophie.

While I scrubbed off the paint and food, I thought I heard the doorbell ring downstairs. I wondered who was visiting. Maybe Leah and Sloane had come over to rehearse with Cam-as-Me?

After the shower, I put my uniform in the laundry. As I was getting dressed in clean clothes, I heard my mom laughing with someone in the kitchen. But who?

I snuck downstairs and into the kitchen, and my eyes almost popped out of my head.

Our surprise house guest was the blond woman.

I screamed.

"Sophie!" my mom scolded. "Is that how you introduce yourself?"

"I . . . I . . . I wasn't expecting anyone to be here," I said.

The blond woman smiled at me as though she hadn't just chased me on roller skates the day before.

"Well, hello," she said, like she was the most charming human in all of O-H-I-O.

The baby hairs on the back of my neck were standing on ends.

Helllpp! I screamed inside.

I didn't know whether to throw this intruder out of our house or grab my whole family and run.

Mom and the blond woman were seated at the kitchen table, drinking tea from Mom's pretty teacups. But what was with all the makeup lined up as if on display?

A cleaned-up Cam-as-Me came into the kitchen next. Her eyes widened at the sight of the blond woman. "I know you!"

"Ha, my sister thinks she knows everyone," I said with a stiff chuckle. If Mom knew we knew the blond woman, then I'd have to explain the bracelet, and at this point, it was all too complicated.

"Eloise, these are my daughters Sophie and Addie. Girls, this is Ms. Eloise," said Mom. "She's a door-to-door cosmetics salesperson, and she has the most perfect timing. I have a Zoom pitch tonight with Los Angeles, and she just rang our doorbell and offered me a mini makeover."

Creepy Ms. Eloise fanned the air, flashing her candy-colored fingernails. "Oh, it was nothing—happy to help. And just Eloise is fine."

"Hi, Just Eloise," said Cam-as-Me.

"And you must be Sophie," said Eloise, practically cutting off Cam-as-Me's sweet hello and looking straight at my bracelet instead of me.

"Hi," I mumbled.

"Pardon her tone, Eloise," said Mom. Her voice and stare turned stern. "My daughters got into a bit of trouble at school today. All three of them."

"We went to the principal's office!" Cam-as-Me announced.

"So humiliating," Baby Sophie said, walking into the kitchen. She eyed Eloise. "Who are you?"

"This is Ms. Eloise. And she's almost done. How much do I owe you for the lip shade?" Mom asked.

"Oh, it's complimentary while I'm still a trainee. I appreciate you letting me test the new colors on you. You look amazing." Eloise held up a hand mirror to my mom's face.

Mom smiled at her reflection and nodded at Eloise.

"Thank you so much. And I'm not rushing you. Please, finish up your tea."

"You're as kind as you are beautiful," said Eloise, and I nearly rolled my eyes. Mom did look great in that lip shade, but come on.

A sincere look came over Eloise's face, and she continued. "And if I may comment on the girls? Whatever happened today, it's nice that their bond is strong enough for them to all go down together. It reminds me of the time my kid sister and I got in trouble in school once. We were never really that close before, but landing ourselves in the principal's office gave us a reason to be scared together, and later, to laugh about it together. We've been close ever since then."

Mom pursed her lips. "Hmmph, that's one way of looking at it."

Eloise gave us another look of admiration. "Mark my words."

The worry lines on Mom's face seemed to relax a bit. And Baby Sophie and Cam-as-Me suddenly looked hopeful that we had someone vouching for us. I tried to wordlessly communicate with my sisters, asking them not to trust Eloise, but I guess my rubbery facial expressions weren't translating. Their eyebrows waggled in confusion when they looked at me.

Eloise smiled sweetly at us all. "I'm willing to bet these three don't get into trouble very often. They look too smart for that. You know, sometimes an adventure gets misread as troublemaking. I'm willing to wager what they had today was an adventure. Maybe not with the best location and timing, but an adventure nonetheless."

Cam-as-Me beamed, and Baby Sophie nodded in agreement. I could even feel the corners of my mouth happily curling up.

Yes, an adventure.

Suddenly, I wondered if Eloise's actions toward Becca had been misread, too. Maybe Eloise was just adventure-seeking in New York. Like, she could be one of those storm trackers, only she tracked the bracelet. For fun.

That didn't sound all that bad to me.

"Thank you again, Eloise," Mom said with a small smile, standing up. Mom showing any degree of a smile after we'd been sent to the principal's office was a win in my book. And it was all thanks to Eloise. "We're going to get ready for dinner now. Sophie, please walk our guest to the door."

As I walked Eloise to the front door, she slowed her pace.

"I hope you weren't too weirded out by my being here, Sophie," she began.

I gave a slight shrug. "Well, it's not every day I run into roller-skating bracelet trackers in my kitchen."

Eloise's eyes were pools of embarrassment. "I apologize for that. There was no good way to explain what I was doing. I wasn't sure if the last girl who had the bracelet communicated with you—"

"She did. And she *warned* me about you." I opened the front door so Eloise could leave.

Eloise planted a foot outside, paused, and turned around to face me. I folded my arms and waited.

"You see, my kid sister who I told you about earlier? Well, she's really sick. She's all I have in this world, and I can't imagine losing her. I know the power the bracelet has, and I want to use that to heal her."

My arms slumped to my sides. The lump forming in my

throat kept me from replying, so Eloise continued in a small voice.

"I'd be so grateful if you would give me the bracelet," she said.

"Oh. Wow. I understand. But I—I can't. It won't come off," I explained through the ache in my chest. I tried not to think of what it would be like to lose one of my sisters, or else I would break down in tears.

"I get that," Eloise said. "But I know one day it will come off. And maybe one day soon. Would you . . . let me have it after then?"

"How do you know so much about the bracelet?" I asked.

"Sophie?" Dad called out from the kitchen. "Come make the salad, please."

I nodded. "Okay, you can have the bracelet when it comes off."

"Thank you! Thank you!" Eloise cried.

The last thing I saw before I shut the door was her triumphant smile.

* 12 *

Practice Makes Perfect

Maybe you got it all wrong about Eloise? I texted Becca from my room after dinner.

She responded right away.

Becca: Who's Eloise??

Me: That's the blond woman's name. She was over today, and she didn't seem half bad.

Becca: You think I was wrong about THIS person???

Becca re-sent the picture I took of Eloise when she was lurking behind a neighborhood tree.

Okay. Point taken. I kept typing:

Me: After talking to her, I think she's been acting bonkers about the bracelet because she needs help.

Becca: You're the one who's gonna need help if you trust her! She's dangerous! ⚠ Don't give her the bracelet! Have to go, my dad is Facetiming me. Be careful!

Me: I will!

I sighed, toying with the bracelet. It was still warm and glowing, and . . . it felt tighter than it had a few hours ago. There was no use wondering what to do with the bracelet when it clearly wasn't coming off anytime soon. I couldn't even imagine how it would come off. It was almost like a second skin.

Cam-as-Me pounded on my door. "Adddieee! Come to my room. I want you to see my performance!"

I did need to see Cam-as-Me's performance to make sure she didn't make a fool of herself (aka me) at the talent show. I opened my door and followed Cam-as-Me into my old bedroom. Baby Sophie was on her bed reading a middle school science book.

As soon as she saw me, she set the book down.

"You need to explain to us what the deal is with the bracelet," she said. "Right now."

I knew it was time.

I showed my sisters my wrist. "Okay. This bracelet came in a package addressed to me on Tuesday morning. There was a letter in it from a girl named Becca who lives in New York City. Plus there was another letter telling me that I could make one wish. So I made a wish and it came true." I gestured to the three of us.

"How can that be?" Baby Sophie asked, incredulous. "There is no such thing as magic!"

"Have you looked in a mirror lately? I don't know what else to tell you. It's real."

"Wow," Cam-as-Me said. "I always knew magic was real."

"Impossible," Baby Sophie said, shaking her head.

"I thought so, too," I admitted. "Until I wished not to be in the middle, and there I was in Sophie's body."

Baby Sophie searched my eyes. "Why don't you want to be in the middle?" she asked.

"Because you and Camille get everything you want!" I said.

"I do not," said Cam-as-Me. "Mom and Dad make me go to sleep at seven thirty! And they won't let me have a pony."

"Well, Mom and Dad put a ton of responsibility on me. But all I *want*," Baby Sophie said, "is to be me again."

"I'm sorry," I said. "I can't undo the wish. The bracelet won't come off."

"Can I have it next?" Cam-as-Me asked.

"I told Eloise she could have it next," I said.

"Who's Eloise?" Cam-as-Me asked.

"The woman who was just here," I said. "With the makeup."

Cam-as-Me frowned. "Oh! Why her?"

"Because she asked. And her kid sister is sick! But anyway, if I don't give it to her, I'm supposed to mail the bracelet to the person whose name appears on the box next."

"Says who?" Baby Sophie asked.

"Said Becca!"

"Who's Becca?" Cam-as-Me asked.

"Can we please focus on the talent show?" I sighed. "We can deal with who gets the bracelet another time. It's not coming off yet, anyway."

"Isn't there something else you need to focus on tomorrow?" Baby Sophie asked, raising one eyebrow.

Oh, right. The make-up math test! I'd totally forgotten. And I'd promised Mom that I'd help "Addie" prepare for it.

"We need to get you ready for my math quiz," I told Cam-as-Me, my stomach sinking. I grabbed my—Addie's—tablet off my old desk. "It's tomorrow, after the talent show."

"Oh yeah, I heard Ms. Frankel say something about that before I took my history lesson nap today," Cam-as-Me said.

My heart sank. This wasn't good. How could I possibly teach Cam-as-Me how to do fifth-grade math in such a short amount of time?

I looked over at Baby Sophie.

"Can you help us, Sophie?" I asked.

She sighed through a sly smile, clearly flattered that I asked. "Fine."

"Thank you," I said, handing her my tablet.

For the next hour, Baby Sophie explained math concepts to us while her little hands clicked their way through multiple-choice answers on online practice quizzes.

We were in Team Asante mode—heads down and focused.

When we were done studying, Cam-as-Me grinned at Baby Sophie. "And now I need to teach *you* the pre-K Barnyard Bop," she said. "For the talent show."

Baby Sophie pouted like a true pre-K'er. "Do I really have to?"

"Yes, you do. You'll love it! It's the most fun ever," Cam-as-Me said, handing Baby Sophie feather props to hold.

My big sister's tiny body deflated as she accepted them. "I seriously doubt that."

"Just do what I do." Cam-as-Me flapped her arms. Next, she leaped around like she was landing on stepping-stones. The girl was walking on sunshine, even with Baby Sophie's grumpiness clouding up the place.

As best she could, Baby Sophie copied Cam-as-Me's movements. But she waddled instead.

I couldn't help it. I started giggling.

"What are you laughing at?" barked Baby Sophie.

I bit my lower lip and concentrated on wearing a serious face. "I'm sorry. Keep going."

"No, I won't." She stomped and crossed her arms. "This is humiliating. Why do I even have to go through with this tomorrow?"

"Because it's the talent show!" Cam-as-Me cheered.

"Can't you find a way to switch us back before then?" Baby Sophie asked me.

"If I knew how, I'd do it right now," I said. Wouldn't I?

Yes, I loved being the one in charge, having more freedom and my own room. But Sophie had more responsibilities than I thought. And I missed my friends. And I was sad that I would miss out on performing in the show.

"Why don't you want to do the Barnyard Bop?" Cam-as-Me asked her sadly.

"Because she's allergic to fun," I answered.

Baby Sophie frowned at me. "I am not. I'm just honest about who I am and what I want! Unlike you! You only do what's expected of you."

My face flushed. "Well, I was honest once, and look where it got us!" I shouted, pointing to the bracelet.

Suddenly, the doorknob rattled, and we all jumped.

"What's all this ruckus in here?" asked Dad, coming into the room.

I instinctively hid my hand behind my back. "We were . . . talking," I answered.

"More like shouting," Dad said. "Come on, girls, it's late. Time for bed. You've not been acting like yourselves at all."

"Understatement of the year," Baby Sophie grumbled as I left my old room.

* 13 *

Showtime

It was finally Friday—the day of the talent show!

(And the math quiz. But I was less excited about that part.)

That morning, the school hallways were buzzing with anticipation.

I couldn't believe that the show was happening and I wouldn't be a part of it.

At least that's what I thought until homeroom, when I heard JJ whisper-groaning in the desk behind me.

"I can't believe Kayla didn't come in today," JJ said.

"She has a hundred-and-three fever!" Mandy replied.

"Now we're one person short for the show," JJ grumbled. "It won't be as good without Kayla."

I froze. This was my chance. I spun around in my seat, and my hand shot up in the air.

"I'll do it!"

JJ perked up. "You will?"

I put my hand down. Way too uncool. "Yes! Totally! Happy to replace Kayla!"

"But you don't even know what we're doing," JJ said, still clearly unsure.

"True," I said. "Can you teach me?"

"Oh, we can definitely teach you," Mandy said. "You're gonna do it? Really?"

I nodded. Hooray! I was in! Maybe my luck was changing. Now I got to be in the talent show.

JJ gave me a high five. "Amazing," they said. "Thank you!"

"Anytime," I said with a huge grin. I was totally winning Sophie a better reputation. I guess you could say I was saving the day. I was kind of a superhero. Look out, Spider-Man!

"So, is it a dance?" I asked JJ and Mandy. "A song? A magic trick?"

Mandy leaned closer to me. "It's a pie-eating contest."

"A what?" I thought I had misheard.

"A pie-eating contest!" JJ said. "Isn't that the most fun?"

"I don't understand," I said. "We're going to eat pies—onstage?"

JJ nodded excitedly. "Yes! Exactly!"

Singing was a talent. Dancing was a talent. Even *baking* pies was a talent. But eating pies? "Is that a talent?" I asked.

"Yes! Whoever finishes their pie first wins. It's going to be hilarious! You, Mike, Alicia, and Jerome are going to do the eating."

Wait a minute.

"What about you two?" I asked, confused. "You're not eating anything?"

"JJ and I made the pies," Mandy said, like that explained it.

"Oh. Okay."

JJ's eyes narrowed. "You're not going to back out, are you?"

"No, no, no. I won't."

"You seriously mean that?" Mandy asked, cautiously excited.

Good question. So I asked it of myself, right then. *Did I mean that?*

Pause.

Why was I agreeing to this, really? Was it because two eager faces were staring at me, desperately waiting for my answer, and I didn't want to let them down? Talk about *peer* pressure. (Get it? Because my peers were *peering* at me!)

For a moment, I ignored their stares like Camille had

when she was skipping down the street outside Paige's. Next, I studied the question as intensely as my big sister, Sophie, would.

What was my why?

My friends' and sisters' opinions used to ring out extra loud in my head. But maybe spending time alone in Sophie's room helped quiet their voices down. Lately, I'd been hearing my own thoughts more clearly.

There was something I wanted really badly, even if it meant doing something wacky to get it: the chance to win a free month of classes at the Franklin School of the Arts.

I wanted to take those songwriting classes as much as Sophie wanted early admission to her dream college. As much as Camille wanted to squeeze the most joy out of each moment.

So, with the intensity of Sophie and the go-get-'em spirit of Camille, I gave JJ and Mandy my final answer.

"Yes, I seriously mean it. I won't back out."

A look of relief washed over their faces.

This won't be so bad, I told myself. I could eat pie. It wasn't a particular talent of mine, but eating pie was definitely something that I enjoyed doing. And my parents were often telling me to slow down and enjoy my food. So maybe I was a quick eater?

"Any chance you have a backup shirt?" JJ asked.

"No," I said.

JJ exchanged a glance with Mandy before replying to me with a head shake. "Don't worry about it. You'll be fine."

They didn't sound reassuring at all.

Gulp! I might have bitten off more than I could chew.

And yes, pun intended.

At twelve-thirty p.m., all the students took their seats in the auditorium.

There were at least five hundred kids. Was I really going to eat an entire pie in front of all these people?

Everyone participating in the talent show waited back-stage. I saw Cam-as-Me standing with Leah and Sloane. And I spotted Baby Sophie with the pre-K class. They were the first to perform, so they stood in the wings, about to go onstage.

Baby Sophie lingered behind the others, looking miser-able. Also hilarious.

She was in full rooster gear—red-and-yellow hat, white jumpsuit, orange-and-red socks. She turned to me and glared. "I am not going out there."

I sidled up beside her. "You have to."

"This is not dignified."

"Please just go on so you don't get Camille in trouble."

Cam-as-Me joined us. "You look great!" she told Baby Sophie. "You are so lucky! I wish I could do the rooster dance."

The "Cock-a-doodle-doo" music started up and the entire class waddled onto the stage in their costumes.

"You've got this." I gave Baby Sophie a little push. "The *cluck* is ticking. Go."

She reluctantly went onstage with the other kids. There were about twenty of them standing in a line, all in various animal costumes.

A loud "Awwwwww" went through the audience.

Ms. Myrtle, the music teacher, played a note, and all the kids started to sing and dance.

"Cock-a-doodle-doo you know I love you?
Oink-oink, do you th-oink about me, toooo . . ."

Their voices were not at all in tune, and their coordination was nonexistent. Arms went in different directions. Kids bumped into each other.

Everyone was singing and dancing around the stage, except Baby Sophie, who was just glowering at her classmates.

Suddenly, Cam-as-Me pushed by me. "Me tooooooo," she cried as she ran onto the stage.

"No!" I yelled, but it was too late. She was already standing right beside Baby Sophie and doing the movements.

The audience, as well as everyone backstage, was understandably confused.

I was—understandably—horrified.

Everyone would think that I—Addie Asante—ran onstage to do the Barnyard Bop! What kind of fifth grader jumps onstage to crash a pre-K number? It made no sense.

She wasn't even wearing a costume!

"Addie!" Leah called.

"What is she doing?" Sloane asked, eyes wide.

What was she doing? Apparently, performing her heart out. Cam-as-Me lifted her hands and swayed her hips as she belted out the Barnyard Bop. *"Wool I ever be baaa-baaa-baaack in your arms?"*

I closed my eyes. I could not watch. This was worse than the flash mob.

I heard cheering and clapping, so I opened one eye to see what was happening.

Cam-as-Me had taken Baby Sophie's hand. Plus, she was kind of leading the kids. When any of them forgot their moves or words, they looked at Cam-as-Me for help. She was guiding them. And she was wearing bunny ears that she must have borrowed from someone during the number.

When they sang their last words—something about a donkey's hee-haw-heart—everyone cheered.

"Wasn't that great?" Cam-as-Me asked, running off the stage.

I grabbed her arm. "No! You were not supposed to get onstage. You are not in pre-K!"

"But I wanted to—"

"Can you please go get ready for your actual number?" I barked.

"That's what I'm doing! Should I wear the bunny ears?"

"No! Do not wear bunny ears!" I cried out.

Leah motioned Cam-as-Me over. "Addie! I can't believe you went onstage with the little kids!" she said.

"That was so weird," Sloane said.

"It was not weird!" Cam-as-Me told my friends. "I wanted to do the dance! And my sister needed help! It would have been weird if I hadn't helped her!"

"I guess so," Sloane said, and I saw Leah nod.

Wow. Was Cam-as-Me right?

I saw Ms. Pinerette lead the pre-K class down the side steps and to the front row to watch the rest of the show with the audience. Baby Sophie looked less miserable now. Maybe she'd had fun in the end?

I watched the next few numbers nervously from the wings. There was a tuba player, some gymnastics, a few dance numbers, and then finally it was time for the fifth-grade acts.

"Good luck!" I whispered to Cam-as-Me as she headed back onstage with Leah and Sloane.

This was it.

I held my breath.

Leah called out, "One. Two. Three."

And they started singing "Wild Ride."

Or Sloane and Leah sang. Cam-as-Me . . . yodeled?

That's the only word I can think to describe it.

She was going off the rails.

Was she making up the words? She'd said she knew

them! I realized that I'd never actually heard her perform last night.

I tried to mouth the words to her from the wings, but she didn't look my way.

I waved my hands, which ended up distracting Sloane and caused her to bump into Leah.

OMG. I needed to take this bracelet off! I needed to switch back!

But the bracelet wouldn't budge. Would I be stuck in this body forever?

When the song finally ended, there were a few claps, but not many.

Sloane and Leah stormed off the stage.

"What were you doing?" Leah snapped at me.

"I was trying to help," I said.

"We didn't need your help," Sloane told me.

"And we didn't need you to steal the show," Leah said to Cam-as-Me. She looked at both of us. "You Asante sisters need to get it together."

This was all so embarrassing.

Cam-as-Me's face crinkled in confusion. "I wasn't trying to steal the show," she said. "I was trying to be amazing! Wasn't I supposed to be amazing?"

She looked genuinely confused.

"Yes, but . . ." I couldn't explain. I needed to focus on my upcoming act.

Pie eating.

As soon as the sixth-grade acts were done, the principal announced, "Now for a very special event. The seventh-grade pie-eating contest!"

The crowd went wild.

A few seventh graders carried out a long table and four chairs. Then they put garbage bags under the chairs and over the table. Was this really happening?

"You should tie your hair back," JJ told me. "It's going to get messy. I have an extra tie if you need."

"Um, thanks," I said, taking it. What had I gotten myself into?

Once we were all seated, Mandy brought out four pies and JJ took the mic. "Welcome to our first ever talent-show pie-eating contest!"

The crowd went even wilder.

Mike was sitting next to me and he gave me a thumbs-up. "You are full of surprises, Sophie."

"Thanks," I said, glad to have a friendly face nearby.

I saw Baby Sophie watching horrified in the audience. I glanced back at the wings and saw Cam-as-Me, Leah, and Sloane all gawking at me.

Mandy continued. "These four contestants are going to race to eat the pie in front of them without—"

Without what?

"—without using their hands!"

No hands? Did that mean no forks, too? Aw man.

"The first one who cleans their plate is the official winner! Here come the pies!"

Mandy set down a pie in front of each of us. They weren't actually pies—just four plates of what looked like whipped cream. I thought Mandy and JJ couldn't be in it because they had baked the pies? What baking? This was just spreading!

"And in case you're wondering," JJ said, "they're banana flavored!"

Okay. At least I like bananas. I could do this. It was kind of exciting! Was it possible I could win this thing?

"You will be disqualified if you use your hands," JJ said. "First one done, raise your arm. On your mark! Get set! Go!"

I went.

I lowered my head down to the plate and debated the best way to do this. Lick? Bite? Swallow whole?

"Wooooooot!" someone shouted from the audience. That got the rest of the crowd on their feet and everyone chanted, "Eat! Eat! Eat!"

I took a big bite.

Oh no. Oh no.

I like banana. But Sophie doesn't. Sophie hates banana! And I had Sophie's taste buds! And this tasted like banana! It was so disgusting. Banana was disgusting! Why did anyone eat bananas? It was like eating garbage! How had I never realized how gross bananas are? BLARGH.

"Eat! Eat! Eat!"

"Sophie! Sophie! Sophie!"

They were chanting my name now! Sophie's name!

As gross as it was tasting bananas, I couldn't stop now. I didn't want to let the crowd down. Not when they were cheering for me. I kept stuffing myself with pie, ignoring the feeling of fullness in my stomach. And the fact that the pie was everywhere. In my eyes, in my nose, in my eyebrows. I didn't stop. I couldn't stop! I had to keep eating! I slurped up the cream and realized that the trick was to breathe through my nose.

And I finished! I raised my hand!

"Jerome is the winner!" JJ said.

Oh, boo. I guess I didn't finish first. But still. I finished! And that was still a GREAT act.

"Sophie came in second," JJ said. "Which I wasn't expecting! Go, Sophie!"

I sat back and smiled. There was banana pie in my eyelashes, so I couldn't see clearly, but I was pretty sure we were getting a standing ovation. Yes! Woot!

I stood up and waved to the crowd.

Rumble.

What was that?

Rumble.

Oh no. The rumbling was my stomach.

The pie, the banana pie! I needed to get out of there immediately. I pushed back my chair and hurried off the stage. I spotted a garbage pail off to the side and beelined right for it.

Out came the pie.

"Omigod," Baby Sophie said, suddenly by my side. She

must have jumped out of her seat and run backstage. "How could you do that? You totally debased me in front of the entire school! I am a dignified person! I would not be in a pie-eating contest! Ever! Ever ever ever!"

"Yeah, I'm feeling fine," I huffed, still holding the edge of the garbage pail. "Thanks for checking in on me."

"You deserve to feel sick after doing that!" she cried.

"That was awesome!" Cam-as-Me announced, jumping up behind me and slapping me on the back. "You did so great! Yayyyyyy!!"

The back slapping threw me forward and almost into the garbage pail.

"Careful!" I said. "You're very strong in my body."

"Sorry, I forgot," she said.

"You can't forget!" I said. "You have to remember who you are now."

"I am so sick of you bossing us around," Baby Sophie said.

"I am not bossing you around," I said. "I'm trying to help! I'm trying to be a good sister. Which is more than you ever do!"

"Why, because I don't let people walk all over me?" Baby Sophie asked.

I stood up and glared at her. "I do not!"

"You do, too!" she insisted.

"Well, I definitely let YOU and CAMILLE walk all over me, and I am done with that!"

Cam-as-Me snort-laughed. "I walk all over you? No way! You both push me around all the time!"

"Oh, please," I said. "You do whatever you want all the time. You literally forced yourself into the pre-K number! But at least people like you. Unlike you—" I pointed to Baby Sophie. "No one likes you! No one at all. The kids at school don't like you, and right now, we don't like you so much, either!"

Baby Sophie stared at me. Then, for the first time in history, my big sister burst into tears.

✳ 14 ✳

Just the Three of Us

Cam-as-Me looked as shocked as I felt.

Sophie never cried.

(Technically, no one would know that Sophie was crying, because Camille was the one with tears streaming down her face. But I knew it was Sophie.)

Onstage, four eighth graders were starting a dance number. My sisters and I moved farther away from the action, into a corner of the backstage area.

"Why...?" Baby Sophie asked through tears. "Why...are you...so...mean to me?"

Huh? "Me? Mean to you? You're mean to me!"

"I just want to help you! I want you to be the best Addie you can be. Which means standing up for yourself. And not being so easily swayed. Yeah, maybe I don't have a lot of friends in my class, but I always do what I need to do."

What was happening? I wasn't mean to my sister! Was I?

I heard a sob on the other side of me. OMG, now Cam-as-Me was crying!

I spun to face her. "What's wrong?"

"You're being mean to me, too! Why was it bad that I went onstage? I wanted to do Barnyard Bop. And Sophie looked scared and I wanted to help!"

"But . . . but . . . you looked silly!" I answered.

"Who cares!" she said, throwing up her hands.

"Why do you care so much about what people think?" Baby Sophie asked me.

"I . . . I . . ." I didn't know.

Suddenly, I realized the truth. I was trying to change my sisters, but maybe I should have been learning from them instead. Maybe Sophie wasn't bossy—she was a leader. And Camille liked attention, but so what? She wanted to dance and have fun. Why should she hide her joy because other people might think she looked silly?

Maybe instead of trying to make my sisters be more like me, I could learn from them. They stayed true to themselves, and I had to do the same. That meant learning to say what I thought and do what I wanted to do, in my own way. Maybe I wasn't the oldest, or the youngest, or the bossiest, or the loudest, but that didn't mean I didn't have a voice.

I just had to use it.

"I'm so sorry," I said to them. "For making the wish. And for not appreciating the two of you."

"Honestly," Baby Sophie said, "this week hasn't been all bad. Hula-Hooping was fun."

"I saw that," I said.

"It was good to be a little kid again. It's not a terrible thing to let loose. Occasionally."

"Wanna Hula-Hoop now?" Cam-as-Me asked excitedly. "Onstage?" Then she paused. "No. It's a school talent show, not a me talent show. Although I do have a lot of talent."

I laughed. Baby Sophie laughed. And then she started to cry again.

"What is it?" I asked, putting my arm around her.

"It just feels . . . so good . . . to cry!" More tears spilled down her cheeks. "I had no idea! Why didn't you tell me?"

Cam-as-Me laughed. And Baby Sophie laughed as she cried. Snot came out of her nose.

"I'm sorry I used to call you a crybaby," Baby Sophie told Cam-as-Me.

"And I'm sorry for saying you have no friends," I told Baby Sophie. "That was really mean."

"What was mean was when I got you into trouble with

Mom and Dad instead of having your back," she said. "No wonder you made that wish."

"Awww!" Cam-as-Me said, throwing her arms around us. "Let's cry every day!"

"I'm lucky to have you two," I said.

"We're lucky to have you," Baby Sophie said. "Big sister."

I laughed and pulled back. "I *am* sorry about making the wish, though. But I don't know how to undo it. The bracelet doesn't come off. There's no clasp!"

I looked down at the bracelet. Wait. There was a clasp! There hadn't been one before! "Look!" I said. "I can take it off."

Their eyes widened.

"And then we go back to normal?" Baby Sophie asked.

I nodded.

She looked at me. "We do want to go back to normal. Don't we?"

"Yes!" Cam-as-Me said. "I like being big, but I'll be big eventually. And I miss naptime. And finger painting."

"I know it's hard being in the middle," Baby Sophie said to me. "I understand if you want to stay the oldest a little longer."

"It can be hard," I answered. "But honestly? I miss being in the middle. I miss being me. Can you both help me take it off?"

Both of them leaned over and studied the bracelet.

"I'll hold it," Cam-as-Me said.

"And I can unhook it . . ." Baby Sophie said.

A gust of wind swept through backstage.

And then it was off.

I blinked. And then blinked again.

And I realized my perspective had changed. I was no longer looking at Baby Sophie and Cam-as-Me. I was looking at Sophie and Camille! And I was holding the bracelet in my hand.

Which meant . . . I was me again.

"It worked!" Camille said, looking at her hands. "I'm me again!"

"I'm myself," Sophie said.

"And I'm me," I said.

The audience erupted in applause. For a second, I thought they were clapping for us, but then I realized it was for an eighth grader who'd performed on the piano.

I heard the principal take the mic onstage. "And that was the last act for this year's talent show . . ."

Wait. "There's one more!" I called out.

My sisters looked at me in surprise.

"There is?" Sophie asked me.

I nodded. "Will you sing with me?" I asked them.

"I have a bad voice," Sophie protested. "And we don't know the words."

"I have a great voice!" Camille volunteered.

I held my sisters' gazes. "You can harmonize in the background. Like this." I sang the simple refrain.

"Together?" Sophie asked.

"Try it."

They nailed it. I smiled and took my sisters' hands.

I hesitated when I realized that this would be Addie's—my—third time onstage today. Would everyone think I was a total scene stealer?

I shook my head. I decided to take a lesson from Cam-as-Me and not focus on what everyone thought.

"Ms. Bryant?" I called, stepping onstage. "Can we do one last number? My sisters and me?"

She looked over at us. Hesitated. "It won't involve food, will it?"

"No," I said. "Promise."

"All right," she said with a smile.

Sophie and Camille followed me onstage. I took the mic and looked at the crowd.

So many people were staring at me.

My hands started shaking. "I'm Addie Asante. These are

my sisters, Sophie and Camille. This is an original song I wrote, called 'Together.' My sisters are going to help."

"You got this," Sophie said. "Ready? One. Two. Three."

I started to sing.

"Where you're alone,

And waiting by your phone . . ."

My sisters joined in for the final chorus.

When we were finished, the room erupted into cheers.

We'd done it. I'd done it. And not just because it was expected of me, but because I'd wanted to.

We bowed, waved to the crowd, and started walking off the stage.

And that's when Camille slipped on leftover banana pie. And knocked into me. And I knocked into Sophie. All three of us were now on our backs *on the stage*.

There was a shocked silence.

Sophie stood up first. And took a bow.

Everyone cheered.

Maybe the Asante sisters were scene stealers after all.

* 15 *

Wait a Second

"How was the math quiz?" Sophie asked anxiously as I met her outside school after the final bell. Camille had already gone home with Dad.

"Great," I said, feeling relieved. "I knew every answer."

"Go, you!" she said, her face breaking into a smile.

I winked. "Well, I had some help studying last night. And you know, it's almost as if I've been in seventh-grade math all week."

"Almost as if," she repeated. Then she gave me a shoulder bump. "Hey, I'm sorry your song didn't win the talent show. It was really good."

"Thanks," I said.

The eighth-grade girl who played piano won the free month of classes at the Franklin School of the Arts. I was disappointed that I hadn't won, but I was also proud of myself for getting up onstage and singing something I wrote.

And for crushing it in the pie-eating contest.

"You're a great songwriter," Sophie added.

"For real?" I said, blushing.

"Yeah. You know I only tell the truth. We need to celebrate!"

Wow. Sophie wanting to celebrate was a big deal. "Can we go to Paige's?" I asked hopefully.

Sophie's eyebrows rose.

"Only if you want to," I added.

She cocked her head to the side. "Funny. Mike Thompson just asked me if I was coming to Paige's again today. Know anything about that?"

"I might," I said with a laugh. "Pretty *smoooothie* of him."

Sophie rolled her eyes, but I could tell she was secretly pleased. "Okay, let's head over. Nice to know you and I are on the same . . . Paige."

I pointed at my sister in pretend shock. "Whoa! You said something punny!"

She took a bow.

I placed one hand to my heart and mimed wiping a tear with the other. "I don't think I've ever felt closer to you."

Sophie laughed.

"Just so you know . . . it's not only Mike I made friends with," I told her. "There's Kayla and Mandy and JJ, too. I know you're probably annoyed that I made friends for you, but I think that they—"

"Thank you," said Sophie.

"Thank me?" I echoed, surprised.

"Yeah. Thank you. I don't always give people a chance, but I . . . I should. Hey, do you want to invite your friends to come to Paige's, too? They're right over there."

I turned around to see Leah and Sloane walking out of the school.

"Sure," I said, waving them over. "'Let's all go . . . 'Together.'" I crooned playfully.

Sophie rolled her eyes again, but this time she didn't hold back her smile.

"Why didn't you tell us you wrote songs?" Leah asked me. She, Sloane, and I were sitting at a table at Paige's with our smoothies.

"I tried to . . ." I said. "But I didn't think you'd want to sing one."

"You didn't even give us the chance to say no . . . or yes!" Sloane said.

"Exactly," Leah said as she chewed on crushed ice from her drink. "It's like *you* told *yourself* no."

I nodded. "Sometimes I feel like you both have very strong opinions and I'm kind of in the middle."

In the middle of them. In the middle of my sisters.

"But maybe it's not about picking between what you want." I looked at Leah. "Or what you want." I looked at Sloane. "But also considering what I want."

"Absolutely!" Leah said.

"Like when you led the flash mob!" Sloane said.

I laughed. "I wasn't exactly acting like myself this week."

"You really weren't," Leah said, shaking her head. "But that's okay. You deserve the same patience you show us, like, all the time."

"Yeah, even when you took over our song at the show . . ." Sloane pouted.

"Sorry about that," I said.

"It's all right," Leah said. "It was sort of funny. I just wish you'd given us a heads-up."

I nodded. "I get that."

Sloane squeezed my arm. "You can make it up to us next year."

"How?" I asked.

"Write us a song that will win the talent show, 'kay?"

"No pressure." Leah laughed.

"On it!" I grinned.

After Sloane and Leah left Paige's, I went over to find Sophie. She was sitting at a table having smoothies with Mike, JJ, and Kayla.

And she was smiling as bright as she had when she'd been Hula-Hooping in the schoolyard.

"Are you ready to go?" I asked my sister.

"Don't go yet!" Kayla said to Sophie.

That's when I noticed the music piping through the café's speakers. "Oh, I wouldn't want to break up your 'Moonrise' listening party."

JJ and Kayla looked at me like adults who warn kids to stay out of grown folks' business.

Right. That was privileged seventh-grade info, and I was (happily) back to being a fifth grader.

"Sophie told me that you like the same music," I added quickly.

Sophie backed me up with a nod before taking out her phone. She texted something, waited a minute, and then looked up at me and smiled. "Mom and Dad say you can walk home by yourself today."

"Really?" I asked, surprised.

"Yup. I told them you aced your math test. And how well you did at the talent show today. And that I want to stay out a bit longer."

I reached down and hugged her. "Thank you, Sophie! See you at home."

She hugged me back, and I left Paige's with a bounce in my step.

I walked the three blocks to my house, feeling the tiredness start to hit me. What a day. What a week. What a wish.

What a—

What was *she* doing here?

Eloise was sitting on my front steps.

Right. Eloise.

I had to give her the bracelet now. Like I'd promised.

She jumped to her feet. "Hi, Addie, is it?"

I nodded wordlessly. I didn't want to say too much because Eloise didn't know about the sister switch. She'd never asked what I'd wished for.

"Do you know where I can find Sophie?" she asked. "I rang the doorbell, but no one's answering."

"She's, uh—she's out right now." I stepped onto my front porch.

Worry lines creased Eloise's face, and I felt bad for her.

I continued. "But I know what you're here for. Sophie, uh, told me everything."

"Oh. Well, yes. Is the bracelet ready? Can I have it?"

"How did you know it was off?"

She showed me the gold bead that she wore on a necklace. "See? This was once part of the bracelet. So it warms up and glows when the magic is working. It's not glowing now, so I know the bracelet is off. I've lost the connection."

"The radar, you mean?"

"I guess you can call it that, yes."

A promise was a promise.

I started to reach for my pocket, but Sophie's words echoed in my mind like a warning.

You only do what's expected of you.

Was I giving this bracelet to Eloise because I wanted to be liked? Was I agreeing just because I found it uncomfortable turning her down?

No. Despite Becca's warning, I couldn't not help someone in need. What if this was Eloise's kid sister's last chance?

I dug into my pocket for the bracelet.

Eloise eyes grew wide, like I was going to pull out a juicy burger. Did she want to eat this bracelet?

I was digging in the wrong pocket, because I pulled out a piece of gum instead. Eloise still reached for it but stopped short when she saw what it was.

"Wrong pocket," I said.

"That's okay, Addie. You won't regret this. My big sister will finally be healed, thanks to you."

I nodded and started reaching for my other pocket. I spotted Sophie just then, crossing the street toward us with her smoothie from Paige's. She waved to me.

Sophie, my big sister.

I froze. What had Eloise just said?

"Wait. I thought it was your little sister who was sick," I said.

Eloise's eyes darted from side to side, as if she was completely caught off guard. She fake laughed to cover up her surprise. "Oh yes, my little sister is sick. But our older sister is so worried."

"But you said there were only two of you." I backed up toward my front door.

Sophie climbed the porch steps, glancing between me and Eloise.

"Did I?" Eloise said. "You must've heard wrong. Now, can I have the bracelet, sweetie?" she asked, her voice growing stern.

"I'm sorry." Sophie came to stand beside me. "I already mailed the bracelet to the next person. It's on its way to Winnipeg, Canada, as we speak."

I shot Sophie a look.

Sophie lied!

Sophie lied?

She never lied!

"Canada?" Eloise growled at Sophie. "You sent my bracelet to Canada? You were supposed to give it to me!"

"I wanted to, but the magical bracelet went magical bracelet on me," Sophie said calmly. "It practically disappeared to the next person who needed it."

"We had a deal!" Eloise screeched.

Eloise glared at us, and Sophie and I both reacted like twin shrugging emojis.

Then, together, we entered our house and slammed the door.

I looked through the peephole and saw Eloise stomping her foot on our porch, furious.

Then I saw Dad and Camille approaching our house, Dad holding Fufu on a leash.

"Can I help you?" Dad asked, frowning at Eloise.

When Fufu saw Eloise, she let out a low growl. She was finally acting like a guard dog!

"Oh, oh, it's the makeup lady!" Camille said, jumping on her toes. "Can you make me look like a rooster?"

"Absolutely not!" Eloise yelled. "Kids are the worst! Argh!" Then she stomped her foot again and stormed off down the street.

Dad and Camille stared after her, confused, then came inside the house with Fufu.

I turned to Sophie and grinned.

"What?" she asked.

"Oh, nothing. Just that I thought you never lied."

"I don't."

"Then why did you lie to Eloise?"

"To protect you," she said. "That's what big sisters are for."

My heart squeezed and my eyes got watery. Sophie noticed, and she gave my back a little rub.

"Thank you," I choked out. "You're a great big sister."

"I know," teased Sophie. "Do you know what else I'm great at? Soccer. Or I used to be. I think I'm going to try out for the team this spring. JJ and Kayla play, too. I kind of miss it."

"You totally should," I told her. "You'll be amazing."

"So will I!" Camille announced, coming over to throw her arms around my waist. "Wait, what were you talking about?"

I laughed. "You know what would be amazing?" I told Camille. "If you finally cleaned up your side of the room."

"Maybe," Camille said with a giggle.

It was the best I could hope for.

"Addie!" my mom said when she got home. "I ran into Principal Bryant at the grocery store. She said the song you wrote and performed at the talent show was wonderful."

"Oh, that's so nice of her," I said, my cheeks flushing.

"She mentioned that the Franklin School of the Arts offers a songwriting class. Is that something you would be interested in?"

I gnawed on my bottom lip to keep myself from shouting, *Yes!* If I said yes, would my mom lecture me about my math quizzes? Or say I wasn't being as responsible as Sophie was?

"Oh, *that* songwriting class . . ." I stalled, even though I was close to bursting.

Mom frowned. "You already knew about the class? It's obvious you want to take it. Why didn't you tell me?"

"I didn't think you'd approve," I finally said in a small voice. "Because it's not something Sophie would do."

When Mom reached out to hold my hands in hers, it soothed the ache in my heart. "I know you and your sisters were just having fun, but you don't need to pretend to be Sophie, or anyone else," she said gently. "I'm sorry if I ever made you feel like you did. Now what do you say we sign you up for that class?"

"Yes!" I finally burst out. "Let's do it!"

"Is there a rooster crowing class?" Camille asked, coming into the living room.

"I'll look into that, too." Mom chuckled and sat down on the couch. I laughed extra hard, because I was deliriously happy. Camille climbed into Mom's lap, and Mom started taking out Camille's hair ties, one by one. Camille collected the ties and placed them in a pouch for safekeeping.

"Here, Mom, this'll keep them from getting lost," said Camille.

"That's so responsible of you, Baby Girl," Mom said.

"I am very responsible now," Camille said matter-of-factly. "Just like Sophie and Addie. I may be much shorter than they are, but I can still help out in all kinds of ways."

"Amen," said Mom.

Smiling, I went upstairs. Sophie was in her room, listening to "Moonrise" on repeat and no doubt studying. But her door wasn't closed all the way. So I knew if Camille and I stopped in to say hello to her, she wouldn't mind.

When I went into my room, I gasped. Camille had finally cleaned up her side of the room! The room wasn't as neat and quiet as Sophie's, but that was okay. It was mine.

I took out the box the bracelet had come in and gasped again.

The label had changed! My name and address were no longer on it. Now there was a new name and address:

Lucy Usathorn
408 Mockingbird Lane
Fort Worth, Texas 76008

"Lucy?" I said. That name wasn't there before. I would've noticed it. And the address definitely wasn't in Winnipeg.

I texted Becca a picture.

Becca: That's the name of the next girl who needs the bracelet! Are you going to write her a letter about what happened to you like I did?

Yes, I was.

And here it is, Lucy. All in one of Sophie's blue notebooks. She said I could have one, no problem.

I hope you'll read my letter before making a wish. And I hope you won't fall for Eloise's lies the way I did. Hopefully, she won't find you now that we've sent her to Canada.

But don't worry, Becca and I are here to help no matter what. I'll add our contact info at the end so you can reach out. In fact, send us a message the second you get this!

We can't wait to meet you.

Best wishes,
XO
Addie

READ LUCY'S STORY IN

BEST WISHES #3:
Time After Time

WRITTEN BY

SARAH MLYNOWSKI

AND

CHRISTINA SOONTORNVAT

COMING SOON

AND IF YOU HAVEN'T READ BECCA'S STORY YET, DON'T MISS:

Acknowledgments

We are so thankful for:

Maxine Vee, who created this beautiful cover and the gorgeous art in this book!

Aimee Friedman, our editor, and Laura Dail, our agent. You are both magicians.

More thank-yous to everyone at LDLA and Scholastic, especially Carrie Pestritto, Elizabeth B. Parisi, Arianna Arroyo, Melissa Schirmer, Abby McAden, David Levithan, Ellie Berger, Rachel Feld, Katie Dutton, Erin Berger, Seale Ballenger, Brooke Shearouse, Victoria Velez, Lizette Serrano, Emily Heddleson, Elizabeth Whiting, and everyone in Sales and in the School Channels.

Thanks to Austin Denesuk, Matthew Snyder, and Berni Barta at CAA.

Thanks to the amazing Lauren Walters.

Thanks to Brittany Schoellkopf, for her fabulous assistance on all the things!

Thank you, Nicole Caliro, for all your hard work and help.

Thank you to all our writer friends and family, especially Bernard, Olivia, Lincoln, Todd, Chloe, and Anabelle. You are magic.

**READ MORE BOOKS FROM SARAH
MLYNOWSKI AND DEBBIE RIGAUD!**

TURN THE PAGE FOR MORE . . .

Don't miss the *New York Times* bestselling series
Whatever After written by Sarah Mlynowski.
Fractured fairy tales for fearless kids!

WHAT HAPPENS WHEN YOUR MAGIC GOES UPSIDE-DOWN?

From bestselling authors SARAH MLYNOWSKI,
LAUREN MYRACLE, and EMILY JENKINS comes
a series about finding your own kind of magic.

Don't miss the *New York Times* bestselling **HOPE** series, cowritten by Alyssa Milano and Debbie Rigaud!

About the Authors

SARAH MLYNOWSKI is the *New York Times* best-selling author of *Best Wishes*, the Whatever After series, and a bunch of books for teens and tweens, including the Upside-Down Magic series, which she cowrote with Lauren Myracle and Emily Jenkins and which was adapted into a movie for the Disney Channel. Born in Montreal, Sarah lived in New York City for many years and now lives in Los Angeles with her family. Visit Sarah online at sarahm.com.

DEBBIE RIGAUD is the coauthor of Alyssa Milano's *New York Times* bestselling Hope series and the author of the YA novels *A Girl's Guide to Love & Magic*, *Simone Breaks All the Rules*, and *Truly Madly Royally*. She grew up in East Orange, New Jersey, and started her career writing for entertainment and teen magazines. Debbie now lives with her husband and children in Columbus, Ohio. Find out more at debbierigaud.com.